Unseen

Stephanie Erickson

For Grace

1.

I was alone at the piano. The music flowed from my fingers to the keys, and then the hammers and the strings, filling the small room. I desperately needed the sense of peace I felt while playing—it freed me from the pressures closing in on me, from the constant drone of people's voices in my head. At least until I hit the wrong note. After nearly six years of practicing *Gaspard de la Nuit*, I still couldn't get it right. But Ravel's piece was my Everest and, someday, I would conquer it.

A knock at the practice room door let me know today wouldn't be the day. "Come in," I said, sighing.

"I'm not surprised to find you here." Professor Peterson quietly shut the door behind her.

I shuffled the sheet music back into order. "Yes, well. I thought it might help."

"How's it coming?"

I glanced at my sheet music.

She walked around me and peered at it through her thick, black-rimmed glasses. "*Gaspard*? Oh, come on. It can't be that bad."

"I don't know what my problem is. The paper's mostly written. I just don't think it's terribly good, or that

1

it represents my last six years of study well enough."

She scooped the skirt of her yellow suit beneath her as she sat in the chair next to the piano. "Maybe you're putting too much pressure on yourself. I know it seems like a big deal at the moment, but years from now, you'll look back and wish for a problem as trivial as your Master's Thesis."

I blinked at her. "Is that supposed to make me feel better?"

She laughed. "Yes."

I harrumphed, and she laughed a little harder.

Noticing my iLs on top of the piano, she reached for it, turning the little device and its ear pieces over in her hands. "Do you remember your audition?"

She paused, but I didn't respond. I just watched as she studied the thing that had kept me sane for most of my life. It was basically a glorified iPod, but it was the only thing that kept the voices out—until I learned to play my own music.

"I don't remember every audition I sit in on, but yours... I think I'll remember for the rest of my life."

The Dohnanyi Recital Hall itself wasn't particularly intimidating. It was the circumstances that were making my hands shake. If I blew this audition, I had no plan B. All my eggs were in this basket: Getting into the FSU College of Music.

The judges, all professors of music at the school, were seated in the center of the auditorium when I walked into the room. I took a breath, letting the music from my iLs calm my racing mind. There were four judges. I'd thought there would only be one, maybe two. I took a breath, letting the music enfold me. It would be okay. I could do this.

I nodded to the judges as I walked past them, then climbed the stairs to the stage and seated myself at the piano.

"Excuse me, Ms. Day. Are you wearing headphones?" It was the judge in the center. She had frosted blonde hair, and a pair of black-rimmed glasses perched at the end of her nose.

I cleared my throat, trying to find my voice. "Well, technically, yes. It's an iLs, to help me concentrate."

"I don't understand," the judge on the end piped up. "What are you listening to? Is it just white noise?"

"No. It's Beethoven."

"It's music. Music like what you're planning to play?" They exchanged looks while an uncomfortable pause settled over the auditorium.

The blonde woman appeared sympathetic, but I didn't need sympathy. I needed understanding. "I'm sorry, Ms. Day, but you can't listen to music during your audition. How are we to know you're not listening to the piece you plan to play? It could be construed as cheating. Please give me the device before you start your audition."

I couldn't move for a heartbeat. They were making me relinquish my lifeline. My dreams were slipping through my fingers, and I was powerless to stop it from happening.

"Ms. Day?"

Nodding sharply, I stood to walk toward her. I turned the iLs off and removed the earpieces. Just like that, I was bombarded by their thoughts.

It looks like an iPod. Did she really think she was going to get away with cheating? I wasn't sure whose thought it was. It was a man's voice, but there were three men, all of them staring me down.

"If you check my file, it should explain about the device. I wasn't trying to cheat, I promise."

The woman looked at me with a kindness in her eyes. "I'm sure you weren't. We just have to make sure everyone adheres to the same rules. You understand, right? It's important to be fair."

Not really, I thought. It *wasn't* fair—I was quite certain none of the other prospective students were mind readers

3

like me. "Sure," I said out loud.

While I walked back to the piano, they were all thinking different things.

How much longer? My back hurts.

This one's going to be a waste of time.

She's chosen some difficult pieces. Let's see how she does. The woman was the only one whose thoughts I could conclusively identify.

This should be interesting.

Sitting down at the piano, I stared at the keys while their voices filled my head. I took a breath, trying to find the music, but their thoughts were so loud. Panic started to rise at the back of my throat.

"Whenever you're ready," one of the male judges said, and sat back in his chair, clearly unimpressed. By the sound of his voice, he was also the one who was convinced I was trying to cheat.

I laid my hands on the keys. *Just play. The music will come,* I thought.

What a joke, that same male judge thought. To shake his thoughts from my head, I slammed the first notes of a Bach three-part invention a bit too loud. Not a great start, but at least it was a start.

The notes came slow at first, but soon, music filled the room until I couldn't hear their judgments anymore. I didn't stop between my pieces, for fear their thoughts would overpower me. Seamlessly, Mozart's *Fantasia in D-minor* flowed forth until I was gloriously lost in it. The sadness, the darkness, the happy triplets all carried me away. Finally, it was time for my last piece. I didn't even pause. I added a transitional measure between the two—a flourish, really—and began playing Brahms' *A German Requiem*.

Before I was ready, the last notes were hanging in the auditorium. The silence that followed was nearly as crushing as the professors' thoughts had been before I started. I stared down at the keys, missing them already.

After a moment, I stood, thanked my audience, wordlessly collected my iLs, and walked out of the auditorium, not hearing a single peep from the judges' mouths or minds the entire time.

"I didn't really think you were cheating," Professor Peterson said, propelling me out of my thoughts and back into the practice room.

"No. I know."

"It was a remarkable audition. Frankly, I assumed you'd be a performance major. I'm not ashamed to tell you, I was a little disappointed when you opted for Music Therapy."

"Yes, well. Performance is great. I love it—don't get me wrong. But therapy... well, that's what got me where I am today. It's something I'd like to be able to do for others. To let them know their demons can be silenced just like mine were."

The professor handed the iLs to me and smiled. "I can't help but wonder how the audition would have gone if we'd let you stay inside your comfort zone."

"Maybe better, maybe worse. It's hard to say." I'd never been without my iLs in a public place again, at least not on purpose. Although I was too afraid to try it again, that experience had proven to me that I could control the voices myself. If only just the one time.

"Maybe that's what you need to do with your thesis and defense. Step outside your comfort zone?" She shrugged and stood to leave. "Just a thought. I'm sure you'll be brilliant. You usually are."

"Thank you, Professor." She always astounded me. Nine times out of ten, she said exactly what she was thinking, and it was always something positive or kind. I didn't know many people as genuine as her.

She smiled. *I hope that helps calm her jitters*, she thought as she left me alone with Ravel's piece.

2

In the end, I decided to pack up and go home. *Gaspard*
wasn't helping, so maybe the solitude of my little
apartment would do the trick. It wasn't far from campus,
and I usually walked. That day was no different.

April was my favorite time of year in northern Florida.
The air wasn't cloying yet, and there was usually a cool
breeze. A last bit of lovely before the oppression of
summer settled in to stay.

My apartment wasn't in the best neighborhood, but it
wasn't in the worst one either. I couldn't hear other
people's thoughts through the thick cinderblock walls that
were filled with iron rods and cement. Silence in my home
was an absolute necessity, and it had taken a while for me
to find an available apartment in a well-insulated, older
building.

My neighbors were all poor like me, either fellow
students or deadbeats who couldn't—or wouldn't—find
work. The lack of income among them kept drugs away,
and that was fine by me. I didn't need that kind of
nonsense anywhere near my life.

In the six years I'd been in the apartment, I hadn't had
many visitors, which was the way I preferred it. The only

family I had was my aunt, and despite the fact that she'd raised me, we weren't close. I had always been more of a burden than a blessing to her, and she never let me forget it. Needless to say, she didn't come over.

My best friend Maddie was my only regular visitor. She and I had lived in the same neighborhood when we were kids, and she'd quickly become my favorite person. She'd helped me move in and decorate, making my one-bedroom unit look almost homey. Six hundred square feet didn't go far, but it was all I needed.

I came in, tossed my keys in the bowl on the coffee table, put my backpack down next to it, removed my iLs, and added it to the pile. Crossing the small space in about eight steps to the refrigerator, I got myself some water and settled on the couch. Breathing a sigh of relief, I sank into the past-its-prime, lime green, hand-me-down couch, and reveled in the silence of my sanctuary. No one thinking about their to-do list. No one wondering if they'd left the back door unlocked. No one worried about tomorrow's meeting. Just me and my own problems.

For a few moments, I leaned my head back and focused only on my breathing, letting my thesis sit in my backpack next to the coffee table. But before long, it was calling out to me. Nagging me, really. Reminding me that it had to be finished in a matter of days.

"By this time next week, I'll be free of you," I said as I pulled it out, along with my computer and a few printed case studies I was referencing. I curled up on the couch, pillow on my lap, thesis on top, and pen in hand. All I needed to do was start marking it up. But I couldn't. The focus just wouldn't come.

I kept circling around to what Professor Peterson had said about this stage of my life being trivial. And she was right. I had funneled so much energy into getting over this hurdle. But the next one was even more important: Finding a job. I had a few leads, but nothing solid yet. Graduation was still two weeks away, and I had enough grant money to pay for my apartment through the end of the summer, which felt like a lifetime away.

I have time, right? I looked up at the clock and saw forty-five minutes had passed already. Feeling a little hungry, I decided to take my work down to the café on the corner and get a salad for dinner. Perhaps it was another excuse to procrastinate, but I promised myself I would buckle down once I was fed.

Who could do anything worthwhile on an empty stomach? *I don't think the slaves in Egypt were very well fed when they built the pyramids.* I grabbed my bag, keys, and iLs, squashing my own personal Jiminy Cricket as I stepped out into the beautiful spring evening.

I had almost reached the café when a shiver ran through me, forcing me to fold my arms over my chest. It wasn't cold out, so I scanned the area for the source—perhaps a fan in a storefront or air conditioning gusting out of an open door. Suddenly, I realized what was wrong... it felt like someone was watching me. Goose bumps climbed up my arms and made the hair on my neck stand on end. I quickly reached into my purse and turned off my iLs, taking a moment to look all around me, but nothing seemed out of the ordinary. Everyone was too absorbed in their own thoughts to notice me, let alone watch me.

Just as I was taking a breath to steady my nerves, a shadow moved in the alley right next to the café. I jumped, but it turned out to be a cat that came out and rubbed up against my leg. I shook my head and mentally chided myself for getting so keyed up over nothing.

The café wasn't busy, so I grabbed a small salad and settled in at a little wrought iron table for two on the patio outside, still feeling a little uneasy. It backed up to Carter-Howell-Strong Park, where you could watch people walking or playing with their dogs. It was one of my favorite places in town to sit and relax.

But relaxation wasn't on today's agenda. Taking a bite

of my salad, I dove into my thesis as my iLs played a soft concerto to help me focus.

I was roughly three pages in when someone interrupted me. "You're concentrating awfully hard, so that must be interesting. Who's it by?"

I jumped. "Um… it's actually my thesis. It's due next week."

He took the liberty of sitting down across from me. With blond hair, blue eyes, and smooth, tan skin, he was very attractive at first glance.

I decided against removing my iLs. *Maybe I'll give this one a fair shot,* I thought. I'd learned long ago that to know a man's thoughts was *not* to love him.

Maybe this would be fun.

3

I called Maddie as soon as I got home that night. She picked up on the first ring, just like always.

"Hey! I was just thinking about you!" My friend's bubbly voice was always a little loud, and I turned the volume down on my phone a few clicks before answering her.

"Guess who has a date Saturday night?"

"Saturday night? Right before your thesis is due? This must be good! Do tell."

"I met Ken at the café while I was working on my paper, actually. He came over and introduced himself."

"I see. And what makes you think he's any different from the string of roadkill you've left in your tracks over the last few years?" She always knew how to cut to the quick. "I mean, the last guy was to-die-for gorgeous, but dumb as a doornail. The guy before that was too selfish—your words, not mine. And let's not forget the old sleazeball…" She trailed off, forgetting his name.

"Hank."

"No." She laughed. "I forgot about him. Which one was he again?"

"Funny guy, but he only laughed at his own jokes."

"Oh yeah. He was a jerk." She paused, reflecting for a moment. "Vinny! That's who I'm thinking of."

I wrinkled my nose. "Oh yeah. He was awful."

Silence reigned for a few heartbeats while we paid our disrespects to my many past dates. "So, I ask you again," she said, "what makes this guy special?"

"Nothing, actually. I have a sinking feeling I will regret this, but he's good looking and I could use a night out."

"I'll remind you of that sentiment if you call me on Saturday night to tell me he's a loser."

"Hey, I'm not that bad."

"Yes, you are. If your Spidey senses start tingling, you're out of there faster than you can say bring the check."

I chuckled. Maddie didn't know I could read minds. Honestly, I didn't think she believed in that sort of thing, or maybe the possibility had simply never occurred to her. She did believe I had an uncanny intuition about people, particularly for pointing out scumbag boyfriends. I'd done it to more than a few unworthy guys she'd brought home.

"Would it kill you to date a guy more than once? Maybe overlook the greenery in his teeth to find out a little more about him on a second date?"

Would it kill me? No, probably not. Most guys were harmless at heart. Crude? Yes. Malicious? Sometimes. Violent? No. Or at least not in my experience.

"What if my Spidey sense tells me he's a serial killer?"

"Was your Spidey sense going off at the café?" Thankfully, she answered her own question before I had to come up with an explanation for why I didn't know his true intentions. "No, I suppose it wasn't. Otherwise, you never would've agreed to the date, right?"

"I guess not."

"So, tell me what you're going to wear."

"Oh jeez, Maddie. Come on. Do I have to wear something special?"

"Absolutely! It's a date, Mac, so by definition, you

have to wear something special. Tell me what you have in mind, and I'll tell you what you should wear instead."

"You know, I wasn't wearing anything special today, and he seemed to like me well enough."

"Oh God. What *were* you wearing? Tell me it wasn't those God awful grey shorts you bought in the little boy's department."

"Hey! They're long *and* they have pockets!" It was hard to find lounging shorts that covered your butt and had functional pockets.

"Mmmhmm." She was unimpressed. "I swear, the next time I'm over there, I'm throwing those things away. I'm not even going to take them to Goodwill. The people who shop there don't deserve to have that horror unleashed on them."

"Hush. I wasn't wearing those. I'd just come from school—"

"Lucky for him," she said under her breath.

I let it pass. "So I was wearing jeans and that purple t-shirt with the sequins on it."

"Fine. Did you fix your hair before going out in public?"

"No. I wore it in a bird's nest on top of my head. You know, how it is in its natural state. Also, you might as well know, I haven't showered in a week, so my hair has a nice, oily sheen to it."

"Mackenzie!" she cried out before she burst out laughing.

"Maddie!" I yelled back, teasing her. "I wasn't wearing the grey shorts, and my hair was pulled back. I'd say I was fairly presentable."

"This time. Let's get back to what you're thinking of wearing on Saturday…"

"Cut to the chase, Maddie. Just tell me what to wear."

"Yay! Okay, you should totally wear that white strappy dress that kind of flows when you walk, the one with the big, pink flowers on it. And your pearls… and those white sandals you have."

"Anything else?"

"Yes, do your hair nice please? Maybe wear it curly or something."

My hair was a beast to be reckoned with. Long, dark, and wild, I always considered myself lucky if I managed to get it back in a ponytail. "I make no promises in that department. You might have to come over on Saturday to give me a makeover to make sure I meet your standards."

"Believe me, I would if I could."

"Hot date?" I asked, half jokingly. Maddie's dating record wasn't much better than mine was. I had a terrible habit of chasing her boyfriends off after hearing what they really thought of her.

"Actually, yes."

I groaned internally. "With who?"

"A new guy at work. He's so sweet, funny, and handsome. I just know you're going to love him."

Oh God, I could tell she was already gaga for him. "Just take it slow this time, will you?"

"I always take it slow! We never go past first base on the first date!"

"You know what I mean. Don't..." I hesitated. "You know, fall in love with him so quickly."

She didn't respond.

"Maddie..."

"What? He's sweet! And funny! And handsome!"

"Yes. You said that," I said flatly.

"When are you coming to meet him?"

I was overdue for a trip to see her. "How about Wednesday? I can come over for dinner with you and your new man, and we can celebrate the turning in of my thesis."

"That sounds amazing! You'll stay over, right?"

"Of course." The drive to Orlando was too long to warrant just going for dinner. "Maddie, what are you going to do if I don't like him?" I asked, trying to gently prepare her for the worst.

She didn't answer right away, and I was worried I'd upset her. Just as I was about to ask if she was there, she said, "Well, I suppose I'll do what I always do—kick him to the curb."

"Right, because you always do that?"

"Oh my God. You'll never let me live that down, will you? One time I didn't listen to you. *Once!*" Judging by her increasing volume, I'd struck a nerve.

I cleared my throat and tried to diffuse the tension. "Yes, well, I wouldn't want you to go through that again."

She quieted a little. "Once was enough. You were right, of course—he was a lying, cheating scumbag."

I decided it was time to change the subject. "Well, I can't wait to see you in less than a week!"

"Oh my gosh, *yes!*"

I glanced over at the clock. *How did it get to be 9:30 already?* I sighed. "As much as I'd love to talk to you all night, I should go. We both have early mornings."

"Work schmerk," she said. "We're overdue for an all-night chat."

"Ugh. I don't think I've stayed up past ten since New Year's Eve."

"That's because you're a grandma trapped in a twenty-five-year-old's body."

"Whatever. At least I'm a well-rested grandma," I retorted.

She laughed. "All right. I'll see you in a few days. Call me after your date on Saturday."

"I will, I promise."

"Love you."

"I love you too, Maddie. Night." I hung up, trying to hang on to the feeling of pure joy she always left me with. It was good for my soul to talk to her, and I went to bed that night still wearing a smile.

4

By Saturday, I was feeling good. I had made one round of edits to my thesis, and was working on round two when Maddie texted to see if I'd started getting ready for my date with Ken.

No. Are you? Was my original response.

Yes! I want to look just perfect! Don't you?

I want to look like me.

She didn't answer that until an hour later.

I hope you've started primping by now.

I still had over an hour before I had to be at the restaurant, so of course, I wasn't. *What do you think?*

MAC! You can't just show up with food in your teeth from breakfast and expect him to fawn.

First of all, what kind of breakfast do you think I eat that could still be stuck in my teeth? Second, isn't it the woman who's supposed to fawn?

OMG. Get ready.

Putting on the dress she'd requested took all of two minutes, so I sent her a picture. *Happy?*

YES! Was her answer. *Now do something about your hair.*

I hated wrestling with my hair. Managing to find a pink scarf that was close to the shade of the flowers on my dress, I tied my hair away from my face. It was sort of bohemian looking, with black curls falling every which way. Luckily, the just-out-of-bed look was in style right now, and it bordered on sexy.

Digging under my bathroom sink, I even found some pink, dangly earrings to complete the ensemble. *Maddie would be proud,* I thought.

Standing in front of the mirror, I assessed the damage. I really didn't look half bad. Thin and proportional. Not too tall, but not too short either. The dress hugged me in all the right places, flowing down to my knees. It really was an excellent choice on Maddie's part. I nodded to my reflection, satisfied with my work.

Snapping one more pic for Maddie before I donned my sandals and walked out the door, I stuck out my tongue just for her. *Tada!*

Lovely! Thank you! Although, you might want to keep the face to yourself.

And how about you?

A picture of her promptly came through. She looked gorgeous. Her red hair spilled down over her porcelain shoulders and tumbled over her navy, strapless dress. The skirt was trimmed with pretty off-white lace, but I was having trouble taking my eyes off her cleavage. She was definitely more well endowed than I was, and she wasn't afraid to flaunt it.

A little daring, don't you think?

Absolutely.

No wardrobe malfunctions tonight, huh?

Haha! No malfunctions here! If these babies come out, it'll be on purpose.

The fact that she was fearless made her even more attractive in my opinion. *Okay, well, good luck with that. I gotta run to the restaurant.*

Have fun and call me when you're done!

With that sign off, I put in my iLs, grabbed my keys, and headed out.

The restaurant wasn't too busy for a Saturday night. I hoped that wasn't a bad omen. Despite the fact that I was a few minutes early, I went inside to get a table. Turned out he'd arrived before me, and the hostess directed me to my seat.

To be honest, he cleaned up well in his baby blue polo and khaki pants. Flashing that winning smile when he spotted me, he stood to greet me.

"You're very punctual," I said as he pushed my seat in for me.

"That should give me some points."

"Should it?"

"Yes! If it didn't, I would have finished watching that X-Files rerun."

I laughed. "Well, I suppose I can give you a point or two for your sacrifice." The menu was interesting, with a wide variety of choices.

"What are you going to get?" he asked after a few moments.

"I think I'll try the Firecracker Bowl. How about you?"

"Adventurous, huh? I like that in a woman. I think I'll try the Citrus Beef today."

"You've been here before?"

"Guilty as charged. I bring all my hot dates here," he said as he folded his menu down.

I bet you do, I thought as I put my own menu on the table.

"So, fess up. What's with the headphones? Are you that into music?"

"Yes and no. Are you just now noticing them?"

"No. I didn't want to ask about them at the café. I interrupted you, so I figured you might have forgotten you were wearing them, but then you showed up wearing them today. They don't exactly compliment your ensemble."

"Uh, thanks?" I bristled a little.

"Your dress is lovely—stunning, some might say. But the headphones distract a little."

"Your backpedaling distracts a little."

"That's fine. You don't have to tell me. It's probably none of my business anyway. Especially not on a first date. You can tell me on date six or seven, okay?"

I wrapped my finger around the wire of my iLs self-consciously. What would he think if he knew the truth?

My first day of kindergarten wasn't like everyone else's. I mean, it wasn't the first time I'd been around that many people. I'd been to the store, of course, and the library with Maddie, but the classroom was such an enclosed space. If there were ten or more kids in the library, I could wander away, feigning disinterest in story time. But there were so many voices in the classroom, and no way for me to escape them.

It didn't even occur to me to be nervous at the time. I had no idea what might happen. I only felt excitement for this new adventure. At first, it wasn't so bad. Maddie and I were the first ones there, and I was used to hearing her, after the hours we'd spent playing together in our neighborhood. The teacher was there too, but I was used to having adults around. But then, more and more and more kids came in.

Wow! This is so cool!

I want my mom!

I think I'm gonna puke.

Do I get my own crayons?

When's lunch? I'm hungry.

Oh no, my desk is brown! I hate brown!

I don't want to stand in line! My daddy said I'm a princess and princesses DON'T stand in line.

I can't—

But I—

That's so—

As more kids came in, I lost track of who they were,

and it became such a cacophony of sound that I couldn't even distinguish complete thoughts any more. I curled into a ball on the floor and covered my ears, trying to block out the roaring train barreling down on me. But, their voices just kept coming.

Maddie came over and put her hand on my back. I think she said something, but her tiny voice didn't penetrate the roaring in my mind.

In the end, they called my aunt and told her I wasn't quite ready for school that day. She was furious about missing a day of work to come get me. She didn't speak to me all day, but her thoughts—the few that I heard—rang loud and clear.

I can't believe what I gave up for this, she thought on the way home, hands gripping the steering wheel tightly. And then, nothing. Her thoughts were always very succinct and to the point. She was the only woman I knew whose thoughts worked that way.

When I told her goodnight, she merely nodded and thought, *She better get her act together tomorrow.*

The next day, I resolved to redouble my efforts to keep their voices out. But I didn't have much luck. I couldn't concentrate on what the teacher was saying over all the noise in my head. It was too many voices for my young mind to handle.

It affected my work immediately. At first, my teacher thought I didn't know how to read or write, and she didn't know how to teach me. But when she asked me to stay after school one day to do an assessment, I aced it. One on one, I did fine.

Baffled, she asked, "I don't understand, Mackenzie. You don't do your work in class, but it's clear you're capable of succeeding. Are you acting out on purpose?"

"No." I didn't like it when adults were upset.

Why am I not reaching this girl? What am I doing wrong?

How could I tell her it wasn't her fault? I barely knew her, so I was hardly going to tell her the truth. I was only five, but I already knew I was different. I decided to be honest, but vague. "I can't hear you."

"What do you mean, you can't hear me? You're hearing me now, aren't you?" *She can't hear me? What does that mean? Is she hard of hearing? Does she have special needs of some kind?* The questions were coming a mile a minute, and I struggled to form a response.

"Mackenzie, do you mean you can't focus?"

That was one way of putting it, so I nodded my head. "Why?"

What a tricky question. And it was worse because she so badly wanted to know the answer—her mind was silent with anticipation. I just stared at her with my giant, brown, kindergarten eyes. I mean, really, she was the adult. Wasn't she supposed to have the answers to all the tough questions?

She sighed heavily and sat back in her chair. "Well, we know you can't focus. That's something."

A barrage of testing followed. The school psychologist recommended a specialist, which my aunt wasn't too pleased about. It was just another expense, another drain on her time; a drain she thought was "useless" and "unnecessary."

The specialist ran a bunch of different tests but, ultimately, the results were "inconclusive." I could've told him why. For some of the tests, he and I were the only ones present. But for others, there were several people watching. He said they were interns, people who were helping him learn about Sensory Processing Disorder, which they thought I had.

Basically, they told my aunt I couldn't process sound the way normal people did for some unknown reason. She'd taken it as another blow. Another burden. Her dead sister had saddled her with a disabled child.

That was when they gave me my iLs, which at that time was basically a Walkman with giant headphones that played classical music. And that was how I fell in love with music.

The music surrounded me in a way I'd never experienced before. The first time I heard it through the iLs, it was magic. The music played loud enough to drown out the voices, but low enough for me to hear someone if they wanted to speak to me.

When it was on, everything but me, the psychologist, and the music melted away. From that moment on, I was officially diagnosed with Sensory Processing Disorder, and I excelled as long as I had my iLs with me.

It wasn't perfect. There were days when my batteries died or my iLs broke. Then, my only recourse was to go home to get some peace. But by the time I was in high school, the clunky headphones were replaced with ear buds, and the Walkman was replaced with an iPod. Life just got that much easier.

The psychologist who diagnosed me became uncomfortable with how reliant I was on the iLs, truth be told. He said, particularly with an early diagnosis, it was best for subjects to wean off the device and learn to cope normally with outside stimulus so they could lead more normal lives. And I was sure that was one hundred percent true for someone who really did have Sensory Processing Disorder. But I didn't.

I was just a mind reader.

Of course, I couldn't tell Ken that. I hadn't told *anyone*. "I was diagnosed with Sensory Processing Disorder when I was five. In a crowd, the headphones help me focus by drowning out..." I paused. I always struggled for the right phrase when trying to explain this to people. "Incoming distractions."

"I see. Well, if you want, we could go somewhere a little more private after dinner."

It didn't take a mind reader to hear the innuendo in his voice. "Let's see how dinner goes."

"Fair enough," he said as the waitress brought our

bowls.

"All right, I told you something personal about me. Tell me something personal about you."

"Well, I don't have any rare disorders, if that's what you're angling for."

"No, but thanks for pointing out that I'm a freak," I said between bites.

"That's not what I meant!"

I smiled. It was fun to see him flustered.

"Hmm. You're good." He jammed noodles in his mouth, perhaps to give himself time to come up with something to say… and maybe swallow his pride a little. "Well, I have four brothers. We all do some kind of manual labor. The oldest owns a moving company. I'm in between the next two, who both work in farming, and the youngest works in construction like me."

"And do you get along with all of them?"

"Why do women always ask questions like that?" he asked with a smirk.

"I can't speak for my sex, but I asked you to tell me something personal. I could have Googled you and found out how many brothers you have and probably what they all did. Which means it doesn't count." I looked at him over the top of my water glass as I took a drink, giving him an opportunity to respond. He didn't take it, so I continued, "Let me break it down for you: Do you enjoy spending time with them? Do you go out of your way to see them? Do I need to spell it out any further for your hard head?"

He swatted me playfully with his napkin. "No. I get it. Yes, if you must know. By that definition, we get along well."

"That's it? That's all I get? I basically tell you I'm disabled, which you apparently judge me for, and you tell me you get along with your brothers? Hardly seems fair."

He threw up his hands. "Fine. I have a big, hairy mole on my ass."

I burst out laughing.

"I see how it is. Now you're laughing at *my* imperfection!"

I shook my head, eating another bite of food, surprised to realize I was actually enjoying myself.

"Your turn. Tell me something about your family."

I rolled my eyes. "There isn't much to tell. My parents were killed in a car accident when I was a baby. My aunt raised me, reluctantly. Now that I'm on my own, we don't see each other." I looked down into my dwindling plate of food, deliberately avoiding eye contact. Whenever people found out about my family, they always felt "horrible," "terrible," or "so sorry" and it made me uncomfortable.

He frowned. "That's kind of terrible."

I shrugged. "Everyone's got some kind of tragedy in their life. I was just lucky that I was young enough not to remember mine."

Just then, the waitress dropped the check on the table.

"Whew," I said. "Right on cue. This conversation was in a downward spiral."

"That's your opinion," he said as he pulled out his wallet.

I reached for my purse to throw something in, but he held out his hand. "I'll get it. It's a date, remember?"

"Yes, well, that doesn't always mean the guy pays."

"Chivalry is not dead!" he insisted.

"We'll see," I said, and he put on a wounded expression as he threw down some cash.

He smiled, a little softer than I'd seen before. "Well, whaddya say? Wanna go someplace a little quieter?"

I hesitated. If we did that, it would be the perfect opportunity for me to take out the iLs to see what his intentions were, but why ruin a fun evening? On the other hand, why go out with him again if he was secretly a loser or a pervert?

Sensing my hesitation, he said, "I promise, we'll just walk and talk."

I tipped my head. "Well, we've already shared such personal things with each other. What more is there to say?"

"Uh oh. I overshared on the first date, didn't I? Broke the first rule of dating according to *Cosmo* magazine." He shook his head in mock shame.

Smiling, I relented, against my better judgment. "I'm game. Where do you want to go?"

"Myers Park is just across the road if you want to walk a little."

"Sounds perfect."

There was no real sexy or graceful way to take out my iLs and put it away. We were a few paces into our walk before I felt assured there weren't too many people around.

He smiled. "So this is an okay spot for you to talk without that thing on?"

"I guess so." I squirreled my iLs into my purse and braced myself for whatever Ken might be thinking. Surprisingly, I found nothing. It never ceased to amaze me how often men were being truthful when they answered 'nothing' to the question 'What are you thinking about?'

But it wasn't long before he let me know what his intentions were. We rounded a corner, revealing a secluded, grassy area behind some trees and bushes.

Perfect. I probably won't even have to do any work. She's been throwing herself at me all night. I bet she's not even wearing underwear, the slut.

I thought about letting it go. Pretending I didn't hear his thoughts. I thought about telling him the food wasn't sitting right or making another excuse. I could have just continued to walk with him without letting him steer me toward that grassy knoll. But something about what he thought struck a nerve, and I didn't do any of those things.

"Excuse me?" I said.

He seemed startled by the volume of my voice and my tone, which to be fair, had changed pretty dramatically.

"What?"

"So, you think I'm a slut?"

"What?" He acted horrified. "I never said that!" *What the hell? This bitch is turning on the crazy a little early. She better be worth it.*

"And what exactly would make me worth it?"

"I…" He paused. Then his face changed. Confusion was replaced with anger, and he closed the space between us, forcing me up against the bushes that lined the path. "Listen, you little cunt. You've been parading that sweet ass under my nose all night, and I intend to get what I came here for." He grabbed my wrist, but I already had my other hand in my purse, feeling for my mace. This date was rapidly climbing to the top of my ten-worst-dates-ever list.

"Is there a problem here?"

The voice belonged to a man who was standing directly behind Ken. He was slightly taller and stockier. With closely cropped blond hair and cargo pants, he looked like he'd spent time in the military.

The same goose bumps I'd felt on my way to the café the night I met Ken spread across my skin. *Were they from Ken, or the new guy?*

I didn't have time to decide because Ken turned, concealing my wrist behind him, squeezing it harder. I continued to dig for my mace while he answered, "No. No problem here. Have a nice night."

I eyed the newcomer, wondering what he would do. *Why can't I hear him?* I could tell he was thinking something, maybe weighing his options, but I couldn't read anything. It freaked me out more than my date did. Him, I could deal with. This had never happened before. Never.

"Who are you?" I blurted out.

Ken glared at me.

"My name's Mitchell. I was just passing by when I heard some rustling. I wanted to make sure you were doing okay." His voice was deep and masculine, but not threatening. I eyed Ken, wondering how he would react.

"Pleasure to meet you, Mitchell." Ken flashed one of those charming smiles he used on me.

Does that really work on other guys?

Mitchell raised his eyebrow.

Apparently not, I thought.

"You know, to be honest, I'm not feeling all that well. I think I'm going to head back," I said. "Mitchell, would you mind walking me to my car at the Genghis Grill?" A daring move, since I couldn't read the guy at all. There was a possibility I was trading one would-be rapist for another, but I'd finally found my mace in my purse, so I was prepared for the worst.

"Sure. No problem," he said.

I turned to Ken. "I'd like to say it was a pleasant evening, but you kind of ruined it. Have a nice life." I tried to wrench my wrist free of his grip, but he yanked me back.

"You think you can humiliate me and leave me in the lurch just because this asshole walked up?"

Mitchell put his hand on Ken's shoulder, but I already had my mace out and discharged before either of the men could do anything. In moments, Ken was on the ground. The colorful string of expletives that spewed from his crumpled frame was extremely satisfying, and I was tempted to stand there and listen to him suffer.

"I bet you regret calling me a cunt now, don't you?" I said to his moaning form on the grass.

Mitchell put his hand on my elbow and I recoiled, not wanting to be touched by a man this soon after my horrible experience. "Sorry," he said. "But we should go. Unless you want me to call the police or something."

"No, it's okay. Let's leave."

We walked back the way Ken and I had come, and before long, I was out of earshot of him, hopefully for good. Blessed silence descended on me, but I only reveled in it for a few moments.

Why can't I hear this guy?

Before I could formulate any kind of intelligent question that wouldn't make me sound crazy—*So, I'm a mind reader and I can't read you. Why is that?*—we were back at the restaurant. I stopped walking when we reached my car.

"Well, you take care," he said, hands jammed in his pockets.

I stood awkwardly for a moment, not sure what to say. "Listen, thanks."

"Don't worry about it. I'm just happy I was able to help." He rocked on his heels a little and avoided eye contact. I could tell he was uncomfortable just from his body language, but I didn't know why.

"Okay, well, see you around."

"Yup."

I hesitated for one more moment. I wasn't going to let this opportunity pass me by, was I?

"You better leave before your gentleman caller gets any more bright ideas."

I frowned. He wasn't giving me much of a choice. And what's more, he had a point. "Okay, well, thanks again."

"Any time." I got into the car, and he shut the door behind me as I fastened my seat belt. I paused before I turned over the engine, but he nodded at me, as if to encourage me to get the hell out of his life as quickly as possible.

I backed out of the spot and left Ken, the Genghis Grill, and the mystery man, Mitchell, behind me.

It only took five minutes to get back to my apartment, but I drove around the block a little, just in case Ken was somehow following me. I wondered if it had been stupid of me not to call the cops on that slimeball.

By the time I got back at a little after nine, the shock had worn off and I was boiling inside. *How dare he?* I thought as I threw my purse on the couch. It landed softly and bounced. Not satisfying at all. I flounced down next to it and kicked off my shoes, shoes that I had worn to try to impress that sorry excuse for a man.

I grabbed my purse and dug out my cell phone to text Maddie. *I'm already home*, I wrote. *That's how good it went.*

My phone rang almost immediately, and I didn't even say hello when I picked up the call.

"Are you okay?" Maddie asked.

"No, not really."

"Why, what happened?"

"He tried to rape me."

"*What*?" She yelled it so loud I nearly dropped the phone.

I heard her new boyfriend ask, "What's wrong?" in the background.

"Mac's date tried to rape her." When he asked if I was okay, she said, "I don't know. I'm finding out. Well, are you?"

"What do you think?"

"I think you're doing better than I would be, because that's just how you are."

"How would you be doing, Maddie?"

"Well, for starters, if some guy had his mind set on raping me, he probably would've been successful. But you on the other hand, I'm sure you fought your way out of it. Get in any good shots to his crotch?"

"No, but I maced him pretty good."

"Why don't you start at the beginning?"

So I did. Starting with how nice dinner was and how well everything was going until we got to the park and Ken tried to force himself on me. I left out the part where I confronted him about what he was thinking, wrapping it up with Mitchell coming to the rescue.

"Sounds like you didn't really need Mitchell in the end."

"Maybe. Maybe not. But he did make me feel better on the walk back to my car." I paused. "To be honest, I'm not sure if I'm more upset about Ken or about Mitchell."

"What do you mean?"

"I just let him go."

"Who? Ken? Are you mad you didn't call the police? Because you still can, you know."

I tried to collect my jumbled thoughts. "Mitchell."

"Yeah, you'll need to be more specific than that."

"He was different. I couldn't read him." Well, that was honest at least.

"Are you talking about your Spidey senses?"

"Well, yeah. I mean, he walked up like he was some kind of knight in shining armor, then when we were alone, he wouldn't even make eye contact with me. He acted like he didn't want to be near me. I kept trying to start a conversation, you know, to find out more about him, but he put me off every time."

"Do you think your probing might have scared him off?"

I paced around the living room and threw the hand that wasn't holding the phone in the air. "I don't know, and it's driving me crazy."

"You're acting like you've never been stumped by someone's actions before."

I stopped walking. This was one of those defining moments. In truth, I hadn't ever been stumped by someone else's actions. When you could read someone's mind, you could kind of predict what they were going to do. But Maddie didn't know about that, so what was I supposed to say to her?

"I'm usually better at reading people, that's all."

"Well, you'd just been attacked! You were off your game! I'm sure that's all it is."

"And now I'll never know."

"What do you mean?"

"Well, I'm never going to see Mitchell again, so I'll never find out what his deal was."

She chuckled quietly, which meant she thought I was

29

being foolish. "Mac, even if you did see him again, you probably wouldn't find out. Maybe he was just interested in getting out of there before Ken came back to the restaurant and decided to start a fight. Maybe you splashed a little mace on him and he was antsy to wash it off. Maybe he was late for his own date, and he didn't want her to see you. Maybe you smelled, and he wanted to get away."

"Maddie!" I laughed.

"Well, you don't know. A million different factors might have motivated his behavior. The fact that you couldn't identify each of them doesn't equate a failure on your part."

But it does, I thought. For the first time in our relationship, Maddie wasn't making me feel better.

"Listen, I can tell I'm not helping, so let me change my tactic. I'm glad you aren't hurt. Also, I'm glad that scumbag doesn't have your phone number or your home address... wait, he doesn't, right?"

"No."

"Good. And in spite of the horrible circumstances, I'm glad you met a guy who shook you up a little. Good to know it's possible, at least!"

"I guess." She was right. I was glad I wasn't hurt, and I would never have to see Ken again. And hey, I had a lot to look forward to—being done with my thesis, seeing Maddie this week, and graduation.

"You know what?" I said. "I think I should just stay away from men for a while. Maybe forever."

She laughed. "You can't! You're coming to meet Bobby in like five days!"

"I promise I won't try to attack you!" he called out in the background.

I smiled. He was a good sport, letting her talk on the phone this long during their date. "Well, he doesn't count."

"And why not?" She feigned indignity. "He's as much man as anyone."

I heard a slap, Maddie giggled, and her boyfriend said, "Don't you forget it!"

"Ugh, you guys are getting gross. Get it out of your system before I get there, but after I get off the phone."

"Duly noted."

"All right. I guess I'll let you get back to it. Have a better evening than I did!"

"Oh, we are."

It was my turn to laugh. "I can tell."

Her tone turned serious. "Really, though, I'm sorry your evening was such a crash and burn. If nothing else, I was hoping you could blow off some steam. You've been so stressed about your thesis, and I wanted this to be a fun night out for you."

"Me too." I sighed. "At least it was interesting, I guess."

"Well, I promise we'll have fun when you get here." She paused. "Hey Mac?"

"Hey Maddie."

"I love you."

"I love you too." In spite of everything, I hung up with a smile, like I always did. My best friend couldn't read minds, but she had a special magic all her own.

5

My thesis was due on Wednesday, and the very nature of time seemed to change in the days leading up to that date. Some moments crawled, like when I spent an hour staring at the blinking cursor on my computer screen. Others flew, particularly when I started to get stressed about how little time I had before my fate was out of my hands entirely. In some of my lower moments, I thought about how much easier it would be if I could control minds in addition to reading them. But that was lazy and unrealistic at best, and devious and borderline evil at worst.

So I marched dutifully to my Thesis Defense on Wednesday, hoping for the best.

I walked into the appointed conference room, where I met Professor Peterson and—by coincidence, I was sure—the other three professors who had attended my original audition for the FSU College of Music. The room itself was relatively small, and it had already been set up for my presentation with a projector, screen, and some speakers. I only had about fifteen minutes to plead my case, and then they would have up to forty-five minutes to question me on my life choices. I swallowed hard, not looking forward to the next hour.

Nodding to all four professors, I tried to lighten the mood. "Just like old times, huh?" I pointed to my iLs, which was securely in place, playing *Gaspard de la Nuit*.

They all nodded and smiled. One of the men, who I now knew as Professor Brown, said, "Yes, and you set the bar pretty high with that audition, Ms. Day."

"Heh. Yeah." *Oh, good, knock them out with an intelligent response, why don't you?*

"Well, we're all looking forward to this," Professor Peterson said, giving me her reassuring smile.

"Okay. Let's begin." I hit play on my computer and immediately bombarded the professors with overwhelmingly loud noises—bombs exploding, fireworks, jack hammers, dogs barking, kids screaming, the list went on. I proceeded to begin my speech, knowing none of them could hear me.

Professor Brown—the one who'd been convinced I was cheating during my audition—raised his hand as his face twisted into a grimace that gave me way too much pleasure. I paused the background sounds. "Yes, Professor Brown?"

"We can't hear you at all."

"Exactly."

"I'm afraid I don't understand."

"This is what it's like for someone who can't focus. Someone who is bombarded with too much stimuli all day, every day. Someone with Sensory Processing Disorder. Someone like me."

I laid another iLs, an old one of mine that didn't work reliably, on the table. "Through the use of this device, an iLs, and the subsequent music therapy, I was able to conquer my demons, focus, and ultimately excel."

"We'll see," Professor Brown said with a sly smile.

Unfazed by his attempt to rattle me now that I was on a roll, I just smiled and kept going. "I was only five when I was diagnosed with my condition and assigned an

Integrated Listening System. School was impossible for me when I started. The noise..." I trailed off, remembering the barrage of voices. I stomped down the rising panic and continued on. "Well, let's just say it wasn't too dissimilar from what I just played for you. I literally couldn't hear the teacher, and I was failing as a result. My teacher was frustrated, and I was non-functional.

"When nothing else helped, they tried music therapy, and it unlocked the prison that had become my mind. Just think what might have happened to me if I'd never been given an iLs, if I'd never been introduced to music therapy. Realistically, I'd probably be in isolation in an institution."

I let that thought soak in. "What a waste of a life that would be.

"Michael Thaut, Ph.D. and Gerald McIntosh, M.D., said in an article, 'Music can drive general reeducation of cognitive, motor, and... language functions via shared brain systems and plasticity.' This is a relatively new discovery, made within the last five years, using brain-imaging technology to see how the brain relates to music. It's now being used to help stroke victims, cancer patients, and amputees, as well as the mentally ill. Who else could it help? Could we use it on the general public to reduce incidents of road rage? Could it be part of the key to unlocking the cure for Parkinson's disease? Alzheimer's? FTD? How far could we reach?

"How many lost souls can be saved with music therapy? All? No, probably not. Some? Maybe. One? Certainly. Does that make it worth it? Absolutely." With that, I was finished. I glanced at the clock. *Ten minutes.* I'd raced through it. Frowning, I hoped that hadn't hurt me.

"I believe it's time to open the floor for questions." *So you can rip my fingernails off one by one.*

"Why is one life worth your entire career path?" Professor Brown asked.

"Because, it is." *Excellent answer.* "What if your granddaughter gets cancer one day? She is dying, and your family is desperate, so you take her to a highly regarded specialist, a miracle worker. That miracle worker saves your granddaughter. But he wasn't always a miracle worker. Years ago, he was a troubled teenager flunking out of school, constantly getting into fights, heading toward a life of gang violence and drugs. Until his desperate parents brought him to me, and I showed him the world of music. He didn't respond at first, but I kept trying until I found something that spoke to him. And he took that message and saved lives with it. That is why one life is worth it."

They were quiet for a moment, and Professor Peterson was beaming. She cleared her throat. "I think that does it, but let's ask some of the obligatory questions, shall we? Where do you see this field going in the future?"

"With new technology, I suppose the sky is the limit. Smaller iLs systems, integrated therapy into the subject's classroom, and ideally, even their homes. Have you seen the iPad apps with a full piano on them?" I pulled out my iPad and opened the application. "It's a complete keyboard in your iPad. And to be honest, it doesn't sound half bad. Someone who needed music would benefit greatly from something like this, from being able to have such easy access to therapy. This is what they have now. Imagine what they will have in ten years when I'm introduced to your miracle worker, Professor Brown." I smiled at him, and he nodded at me. It was the most encouragement I'd ever gotten from him.

Then his expression turned hard. "I only have one question left, Ms. Day."

"Fire away," I said, trying to sound confident.

"What have you done to deserve this Master's Degree?"

"I think a better question is what will I do with the degree?" He sat back in his chair, his satisfied expression only partially hidden by his enormous grey beard. "And the answer to that is: I plan to unlock the future by freeing the minds of those who are imprisoned."

"All right. Does anyone else have anything further to ask?" The other three professors shook their heads. "Then I see no point in wasting everyone's time here." Professor Brown stood and reached out his hand. I stared at it in disbelief. "Good work, Ms. Day. I will see you on Saturday at graduation."

6

Euphoric. That was the only way to describe how I was feeling. Euphoric. That feeling didn't fade either, not even with the daunting task of meeting and evaluating Maddie's boyfriend ahead of me.

I knocked on her door right on time with a smile on my face and a booming song in my heart.

She opened it with arms spread wide. "Hi, my favorite smartie pants!" For a third grade teacher, she was remarkably strong. She lifted me off the ground, and we spun together.

I was breathless when she put me back down.

"How do you feel?"

"Excited! Weightless. Scared."

She laughed. "Well, you can be scared after graduation. This weekend is for celebrating!" She ushered me into the living room.

Maddie's apartment was small like mine. There was a living room, kitchen, bedroom, and bathroom, and that was about it. But, she'd made into a place you'd actually want to spend time in, not just a place to sleep. Earth tones on the walls made it soothing, but brighter accent pieces kept your eyes interested.

"The place is looking great Maddie. You should've been a designer."

She chuckled wistfully. "Maybe in another life. One with more money."

A man popped his head around the corner. Bobby, it had to be. "Do I get to be in this new life with more money?" His dark hair dangled down passed his shoulders as he leaned out of the kitchen. I'd never pictured Maddie with a long-haired guy before. It was an adjustment.

She walked over and kissed his cheek. "Of course you do. Now keep stirring that. Don't let it settle." He disappeared again obediently enough.

In a matter of minutes, Maddie had dinner for three set out on a table meant for two. We sat elbow to elbow, sort of staring at each other for a moment.

"Well, I don't know about you, but I'm starving," I said as I reached for the bowl of pasta.

Maddie took some bread and passed it to Bobby. Adoration poured from her eyes, but he wasn't looking at her. He was looking at his phone.

Damn it. They're down by two, he thought.

I frowned. "So, Bobby, what exactly do you do? Maddie said you met at school."

"Yeah." He set his phone on his leg, out of sight, but still accessible. I didn't approve. "I'm the new P.E. coach."

"How do you like the school?"

His green eyes snapped up to mine, a trace of irritation in them. Despite the negativity coming from him, I could see why Maddie was attracted to him. As a rule, I didn't entertain guys with nicer hair than mine, but his eyes were very striking against his pale skin and dark hair. "It's good. And hey, the people I work with aren't half bad." He shrugged, and Maddie beamed.

I watched the two of them for a moment. Maddie's hand was resting on the table at an angle that looked slightly uncomfortable for her, but she didn't notice. Her thoughts were totally focused on him.

I hope Mac sees how wonderful he is. How could she not? Look at him. She was just barely touching his hand. He sat back to glance down at his phone and, in doing so, moved away from her. She reached for her wineglass and even managed to convince herself it was her idea to do it.

"How long have you been teaching?"

He sighed, clearly annoyed to be pulled away from his phone. "This is my third year," he said, jamming some pasta into his mouth. "Mmm. Man, Maddie, this is really good. Way better than that slop you tried to feed me the other day." He looked at his plate when he said it, so he didn't see the way she was beaming from his backhanded compliment.

"I always said she could've been a chef," I said through my teeth, shocked at the fact that Maddie had completely ignored his barb.

"Chef, designer, teacher. I'm a triple threat."

Dinner continued on that way, and I was fairly unhappy with Bobby by the end. While we were clearing the dishes, he parked in front of the TV. Maddie took the opportunity to interrogate me.

"Well! What do you think?"

"Maddie." I hesitated, searching for the words that wouldn't break my best friend's heart. I'd never successfully found them before, but it hadn't stopped me from searching.

"You don't like him, do you?" Her voice turned quiet as disappointment smothered her normal jubilance.

"It's not that I don't like him. He's perfectly pleasant."

"So..."

"I don't like how he treats you."

"What do you mean? You heard him compliment my dinner! He loves me!"

"Not as much as he loves himself." There. Harsh, but true.

Her face contorted like I'd smacked her, and her mind started whirring with emotions—panic, disappointment, anger. "What? What exactly do you mean by that?"

"I didn't mean to make you mad. Maddie, you are always the one doing the fawning. Don't you think you deserve to be the source of someone's infatuation? I do. This guy ogles his phone more than he does you." *And it doesn't take a mind reader to see that.* "He just seems a little indifferent."

She can't be right, can she? Does he really not love me at all? How can that be? Her mouth formed a thin line, and I knew our conversation was over.

"I'm sorry," I said and walked out into the living room, where Bobby was already watching TV, giving her a moment to collect her thoughts.

I sat down on the other end of the couch, leaving a cushion of space between us. It was still too close for my comfort. He didn't even acknowledge I was there. Knowing Maddie would need a few minutes to cool down, I didn't really make an effort to interact.

Before long, a Victoria's Secret commercial came on, and his mind exploded. *Yeah, that's what I like to see. Wonder what she's like in bed. Probably a firecracker. Oh, yeah, bend over a little more.*

I couldn't listen to any more of it. "Bobby, I'm going to cut right to the chase. Do you have any feelings for Maddie? Or is she more like a placeholder for you?"

"What? Jesus, Mac. That's a little out of line, don't you think?"

"No, I don't. Otherwise, I wouldn't have said it."

"Look, I barely know you, so I don't think this is an appropriate conversation for us to be having."

"I really couldn't care less about you, your feelings, or how uncomfortable you are. I care about Maddie. Apparently a hell of a lot more than you do."

"Whatever," he said, shifting until a little of his back was to me.

Oh, like hell was that going to make me drop the subject. "'Whatever' isn't much, as far as declarations of love go."

"Look, bitch, my feelings for Maddie are none of your business."

"And that's where you're wrong—"

Maddie picked that moment to make her entrance back into the living room.

"Where the hell have you been?" Bobby demanded.

Her eyes darted from him to me.

I glared at him. "How dare you talk to her that way! If you have a beef with anyone, it's me, not her."

"Maddie, your 'friend' here is being a total bitch. I think she should probably go." He said it so confidently, and why wouldn't he? She'd always been at his beck and call before.

"I'm sorry you feel that way, Bobby," she said in a quiet but determined voice, "but it's not her that I'm going to ask to leave."

"What the hell happened here tonight? You girls just totally ganged up on me! Are you lesbians or something?"

I laughed. "You wish."

He finally stood up and went to Maddie. "Listen, Maddie. Mac is just jealous. Her own date was a total sleazeball, and she's taking it out on us. She doesn't want to share you."

Impressive. "Wow. That's some fast talking, Bobby."

He reached for her hands for the first time, trying to salvage what was left of their 'relationship.' *But why?* Maybe it was a pride instinct. He seemed like the kind of guy who liked to do the dumping rather than the other way around.

Maddie, on the other hand, was thinking about everything at once. *What a snake. I can tell he's lying. Mac isn't like that. She's never been jealous of me, except maybe about my boobs. I do have great boobs. Oh God, he's reaching for me. Is that the first time tonight he's touched me on purpose? That can't be right. I must be forgetting something. Surely, he kissed me when he came in. Or did I kiss him? Did I even give him a chance to kiss me? What is wrong with me?*

He leaned in close to her. "Maddie, come on, please?"

41

She took a step back, but not far enough to escape his embrace. "Please what? Please be a little more of a doormat, so you can keep walking all over me?"

"No! I'm not walking all over you! She's putting words in your mouth!" He jabbed his finger in my direction, and I just shook my head.

He's losing and he knows it, but he's having trouble believing it. "Your arrogance is astounding, Bobby," I said.

He rounded on me and got right in my face. I held my ground and stared back at him without flinching. We were practically nose to nose. "You probably deserved whatever that guy gave you last weekend."

"Get out," Maddie said quietly from across the room.

"Fine," he said, snatching his keys off the end table. "You're a lousy lay anyway."

"Very mature of you," I got in just before he slammed the door.

Maddie slumped in the kitchen doorway, withering under his cruelty. I rushed over and hugged her while her mind raced with why's, how-could-he's, and how-could-I's. I wasn't sure how long we stood there, but when her mind was finally quiet, either at peace or numb, I led her to the couch and covered her with the blanket that was draped across the back. Quickly, I retrieved a pint of ice cream and two spoons from the kitchen and came back to sit next to her.

Wordlessly, she took the spoon and indulged, the gratitude pouring off her washing over me like a warm breeze. I smiled in spite of myself.

"You know, this isn't even good without sprinkles," I said.

"Don't you dare you even joke about ruining this gourmet ice cream with sprinkles! They'd make it look like clown puke."

I looked at her from over my spoon. "I'm sorry Bobby turned out to be such a jerk."

"Me too." She paused as she sucked ice cream from

her spoon. "Do you think we'll ever get married?"

"To the right people?"

"Well, ideally, yes."

Somehow, I couldn't imagine myself getting married. Constantly knowing every single thought of your significant other didn't seem like it could be healthy for a relationship. "I don't know about me, Maddie. I really don't. But I have high hopes for you. There's someone out there who will adore you even more than I do. Then we'll know he's the one."

She scooted closer to me and rested her head on my shoulder. "I'm not sure it's possible for someone to adore me more than you do."

"Of course it is! We just haven't found him yet."

We sat in silence, eating about half of the ice cream while I listened to Maddie stew. Suddenly, she flipped like a light switch.

"Enough." She tossed her spoon into the carton I was holding. "We're going to celebrate your thesis presentation tonight, not wallow in our bad luck with men."

"All right. What do you want to do? Get wild?"

"Maybe. You know it's open mic night at the Muldoon."

I paused wistfully. "It's been a long time since we've done open mic night."

"Did you bring your guitar?"

"Of course I did."

"I'm game if you are."

"Okay, let's go."

Open mic night had been a staple of our teen years. Every weekend, we'd found somewhere to play together—I would strum my guitar and Maddie would sing. We even had a small following of people who'd come and see us if we gave them enough notice. But most of the time, we'd decide where to play at the last minute, much like we'd done tonight.

Muldoon's was busy for a Thursday night, and just gearing up to start the festivities, so I put our names in while Maddie got us a couple of drinks.

The first few acts weren't half bad, but I wasn't surprised. Orlando had a lot of talent, talent that probably wouldn't go any further than Muldoon's.

I watched Maddie tap her foot to the music, wondering what she was thinking about, and if she'd been able to let Bobby go already. In the busy crowd, my iLs prevented me from checking in on my beloved friend. But maybe that was best. We all deserved some privacy in our dark moments.

Four or five acts in, they called our name. I grabbed my guitar and followed Maddie on to the stage. We hadn't even talked about what we wanted to do, but I wasn't nervous. No matter what I played, she would be brilliant.

I plucked out the first few notes of *California Dreamin'*, and she smiled wide—it was her favorite song. She started singing, and her performance was flawless. Her voice was deeper than you might think, with a richness to it that I loved. On the stage, standing next to my best friend, I felt at home. Even though we weren't playing anything complicated like *Gaspard de la Nuit*, we were still living the music. And as I looked down at the faces in the crowd beneath us, I could tell they were living it too. Heads bobbed, feet tapped, lips moved along with Maddie, and at the end of our song, everyone in the house was on their feet, demanding an encore.

As I scanned the crowd, I spotted a familiar face. Mitchell was there in the crowd, with a dark and handsome friend whispering in his ear. *What the hell is he doing here? We're miles from where I saw him last.*

Maddie noticed my startled expression and raised her eyebrows at me. I looked over at her and smiled. "Just like old times," I yelled loud enough for her hear me over the applause.

When I looked back, they were gone. I convinced

myself that I'd imagined it—that it had been some doppelganger of Mitchell's rather than Mitchell himself—and a mixture of relief, disappointment, and unease settled in my gut.

7

I went home on Friday, and then picked Maddie up at the train station Saturday morning for my graduation.

On the drive to my school, she asked me a question she'd been chewing on for quite some time. I was kind of relieved when she finally spit it out—I was sick of listening to her go over it again and again in her head. "Is your aunt meeting us here?"

"No, actually, when I tried to call her with the details, her phone had been disconnected. Who knows where she is. Finally free of me, I suppose." I stared straight ahead, trying not to give any emotion away on my face. Truth was, despite our rocky relationship, I'd hoped she would be there. She was my only true family, and some twisted part of me wanted her to be proud of my accomplishment. But she hadn't come when I'd walked for my bachelor's degree either, so her absence wasn't surprising. I was trying hard not to let my irritation progress to hurt.

"What? Jesus, Mac. Are you worried about her?"

I snorted. "No. She always said I was a drain, nothing but a waste. She's just doing her thing now."

Maddie couldn't let it go. "But, don't you think she wanted to see you walk at all?"

"Maddie, if she cared, she'd be here."

I thought back to the day my acceptance letter from FSU had arrived. It had been so exciting to have the path to my dreams laid out before me. But my aunt had been completely indifferent, and I'd been too young to know better than to let her steal my happiness.

She skimmed my acceptance letter with cold grey eyes for no more than thirty seconds before lowering it. "What am I supposed to do with this?"

"I…" I stammered, her reaction knocking the wind from my sails.

"Is it going to cost me anything?"

I stood up a little straighter. "No. Not if you don't want it to. I'll find a way to do it without you."

She threw the letter down onto the table between us. "Fine," she said and went back to reading the newspaper. She didn't waste even a single thought on the letter. I heard nothing in her mind but the words from the story she was reading.

It wasn't the first victory that she hadn't shared with me, but it was my biggest. All at once, any remaining attachment I had to her was severed.

"I hate you." It wasn't much more than a whisper, but I knew she'd heard me.

Her cold gaze fell on me, but this time I was so hot with rage, I didn't feel it. "And how do you think I feel about you, Mackenzie? You've stolen everything from me." *My whole life has been wasted on you,* she thought as she glared at me. And then, silence.

Of course, hate was a strong word that could be thrown around too often by teenagers. But at that moment, I meant it. And thinking back on our encounter, I didn't regret my words. She made my life very difficult for those first few years on my own. I'd needed to scrape and scrounge to afford anything, even food, while she lived

47

relatively comfortably in her middle-class home. I mean, she wasn't taking luxury trips every weekend, but she did have clothes on her back and food on her table. I usually went over to Maddie's on the weekends just to get a good meal.

I sighed as I pulled into a parking space in front of the auditorium. All of that was behind me. My aunt could be part of my life or not, as she chose. I had decided long ago not to waste any more tears on her. Besides, I had a world of opportunity ahead of me. Why waste time looking back?

The ceremony was a little long this time around. My third time walking for a diploma was a bit bittersweet. All the other times, I knew there was more school ahead. But this time, as Professor Peterson smiled and handed me the dummy diploma, I felt like she was passing the baton, and I was gearing up for the longest leg of the relay: Life.

After the ceremony, Maddie and I went to dinner to celebrate. It was a fairly nice sit-down restaurant, and Maddie insisted it would be "her treat." I felt guilty about allowing her to pay, since she still couldn't afford a car, but she was adamant.

She raised her glass. "To the graduate and the next phase of her life!"

I clinked my wine against hers. "To the next phase!"

She took a sip. "Speaking of which, any leads yet?"

"No solid ones. I've got applications in with Leon and Orange counties, and a few with the surrounding counties too."

"With the county? What does that mean?"

"It sounds like I'd be a roaming therapist for all the schools in the county. It's not really in the state budget to have a single therapist per school, which is what I'd really like to do since it would let me focus on individual kids. This way, I'll have thousands of kids to sort through. It'll be a lot."

She took a bite of pasta. "Mmm. But, it'll be work."

"Yes. It'll be work."

"So nothing in the private sector?"

"Not yet, but I'm hopeful. I have a fair amount of feelers out. Can you imagine if I landed a job like that? Think of the resources I'd have at my disposal."

"Not to mention that the pay would be much better. You know, it'll take forever for you to save up enough to own your own practice if you work for the school system for a long time."

"Yeah, I know. If I get a job with them, I'll have to change my mindset a little. It would be a challenge. But, I always like a challenge. As long as I could still do some good, I'd be happy."

Maddie raised her glass to that, with one last sip of wine inside. "To doing some good!"

I smiled. "To doing some good."

I walked out to the car while Maddie was in the bathroom, thinking I'd get the air started.

The overwhelming feeling that I was being watched made me miss a step. Goose bumps that were becoming too familiar formed along my arms, and the hair on the back of my neck stood up. I scanned the area, and my eyes landed on a guy about a hundred paces ahead of me. Leaning against the streetlight, he was looking right at me with a bit of a smirk on his face. It was the guy from Muldoon's, the one I'd seen with Mitchell. I couldn't believe it.

Discreetly, I reached into my purse and turned my iLs off, to see if he was a threat or if he was just being a guy. I kept walking toward him, but I still didn't hear anything. Forgetting the potential threat, I stared openly at this person I couldn't read—the second in a matter of weeks. He stared back, the smirk never leaving his face.

Who were these guys and why did they seem to be following me?

As I got closer, I realized his expression wasn't threatening. In fact, he was gorgeous. The attraction was immediate and overwhelming in a way that caught me off guard. Only a little taller than I was, he had dark, wavy hair, chocolate eyes, and beautiful olive skin. He was dressed in loose-fitting jeans and a T-shirt that read, "Can you hear me now?"

I chuckled when I read it. Just as I was about to open my mouth to say hello to him, he moved to leave, walking in the opposite direction of me. When he brushed past me, we almost touched. My skin tingling at the mere thought of making contact with him, I stopped in my tracks and watched him go. Never had I been so attracted to, and confounded by, anyone in my life, let alone a complete stranger. It made him all the more intriguing.

I nearly called out to him as I watched him walk away, but my mind was still struggling to form an appropriate comment when he rounded the corner and disappeared.

Had I suddenly lost the ability to read minds? I had gone through my entire life with the ability to hear everyone, whether I wanted to or not, and now I'd met two men I couldn't read at all. On top of that, I couldn't shake the feeling that the guy had *known* I couldn't hear him. The image of his shirt flashed through my mind again.

I dug around in my purse for my keys. My hand landed on what felt like a business card. I pulled it out, thinking it was just some junk I'd jammed in there, but I didn't recognize it at all.

In the center of a completely white card, it said *Unseen*. On the back was an address. That was it. Simple. Mysterious. Irresistible.

I flipped the card over several times as I settled myself in the driver's seat, each time irrationally hoping I'd find more information.

Unseen. What the heck does that mean? Is it some cult or something? I jammed the keys in the ignition and turned the air on full blast with one hand as I continued to turn the card with the other. Where had I even picked it up? It seemed like the sort of thing I'd remember. Could he have dropped it in my purse when he walked by? The thought was as exciting as it was alarming.

I dug my phone out of my purse and typed the address on the back of the card into Google maps. It wasn't all that far from here, maybe five minutes away, and it appeared to be in the industrial district.

What could be in the industrial district? I wondered.

"Predators who lure women with strange, uninformative business cards, that's what." It was exactly what Maddie would say to me if I gave her the chance. Quickly, I glanced around for her. I didn't want her to catch me with the card. It would just lead to questions. Ones I didn't have answers to at the moment. Questions that would inevitably lead me to the address on the back of the white card, whether it was the smart decision or not.

I couldn't let this go. What if this was my chance to find out more about these strange men I couldn't hear? I couldn't possibly waste this second chance after the way I'd blown my opportunity to question Mitchell.

Hurriedly, I jammed the card back into my purse and tossed it on the floor of the passenger's side before Maddie came back.

I needed answers. And I was going to get them.

8

Maddie and I parted ways in the morning. I'd originally asked her to stay all day on Sunday, but she wanted to get back to catch up on some grades and lesson plans.

"Some of us aren't lucky enough to be done with school already," she said as she loaded her things into my car. I'd offered to drive her home, but she'd insisted on taking the train, saying she'd use the time to get a head start on her grading.

Once we got to the station, I helped her carry her bags to the platform and gave her a hug. "Have a safe trip home. I'll call you soon."

"You better. We need to plan our summer. It might be your last summer of freedom!"

"God willing."

"Congratulations, Mac," she said, holding my hand for a few more moments. "I'm so proud of you."

Not many people had ever said those words to me and meant them. Lord knows my aunt never said anything that might be misconstrued as praise or encouragement. Professor Peterson had, which made me feel good in a hey-I-pleased-my-mentor kind of way, but this was different. This was the kind of fulfillment you got when someone in your family saw you struggle, stood by you through it all, and watched you come out on the other side.

I managed a weak smile. "Thanks."

She smiled, and then broke the emotional tension quickly. "Oh, please. Don't tell me the ironclad box that holds Mackenzie Day's emotions has been cracked by one small compliment."

I laughed and pushed her. "No. Certainly not a weak compliment like that one."

"That's what I thought." She hugged me one last time. "I'll see you soon."

"Can't wait," I said.

I didn't go home. Instead, I typed the address on the back of the mysterious, white card into my phone and followed the instructions from my GPS app.

After about twenty minutes of driving, my phone chirped, "Arriving at address 1817 Capital Circle Northwest, on the left."

"This can't be right," I said to no one in particular. The building I parked in front of was long and narrow, with metal, rolling doors all along the front. I walked to the door marked 1817, but it seemed vacant. There were no signs or lights to indicate any form of life existed in the building. My car was the only one in the lot.

I looked at my watch. 11:30 am on a Sunday. Maybe they were closed. My phone chimed as I walked back to my parking spot.

It was a text from Maddie. I leaned against my car to read it. *Grading papers sucks. Wish you were here. What are you up to? Get home okay?*

What could I tell her? *Oh, I'm just at an abandoned warehouse all by myself, waiting to be murdered.*

Laughter interrupted my thoughts. "I don't think anyone's going to murder you out here in broad daylight. Although, I've been wrong before."

Startled, I whirled around to find the gorgeous guy from the restaurant leaning against the metal door. So, I'd guessed correctly—he *was* the one who'd put the card in my purse. I wasn't sure if I was excited to see this handsome man again, or if the fog of mystery surrounding the whole situation made me leery of him. But as I looked at him, his eyes crinkled with laughter, excitement was winning.

Realizing I'd been staring at him for a beat too long, I spit out the first thing that came to mind.

"Where did you come from?" I could have asked so many questions. *Who are you? Why were you at Muldoon's that night? How come I can't read your mind? Did you just read* my *mind? Can I be your girlfriend forever?* Apparently, my mind had gone for the least pressing one.

"Inside."

"Okay, well, I assumed you came from inside. I mean, I know you didn't teleport."

He flashed the same sly smile that had slayed me the night before, making it very difficult for me to keep my wits. "Do you want to come in?"

To my life, my arms, my bed? I mentally finished for him. I thought I heard him cough, but I couldn't be sure.

I took a deep breath, struggling for composure. "I don't know. This is all very creepy and cloak and dagger. Are you going to pull my fingernails off or something?"

"Huh. No one's ever asked me that before."

"Right. Not reassuring me."

He chuckled, and the sound made my knees weak.

"No, we won't pull your fingernails off."

"We?"

"Well, I didn't bring you here for a one-on-one conversation, if that's what you thought."

"I know. It's not a date." *Dear God, why did you say that? He wasn't implying it was a date. Idiot.*

"Okay," he said. "Well, I'm going back inside. You can chill in the parking lot if you want, or you can come with me to find out a bit about who we are. It's not really a life-or-death choice."

My phone chimed again, but I ignored it. "I'm coming."

He shut the outer glass door behind him, then pulled a heavy metal door down behind that, and turned a giant lock on it, almost like a bulletproof safe.

Once inside, we almost immediately descended a staircase. "Okay, the metal door and basement thing aren't exactly making me feel better about this whole situation. Is all that so no one can hear me screaming?"

"Didn't you see how empty the parking lot was?" he said, turning to smile at me. "Who would hear you?"

"Man, I hope I get to look back on this and laugh at your jokes, but right now, they're creeping me out in a big way."

He stopped two steps from the bottom. For a split second, I thought he was going to off me right then and there. Then he burst out laughing. "Would you relax? We're not going to kill you!"

"I…" I paused, confused. "I don't think I said anything about that."

He descended the last two stairs, and I followed. "Not in so many words."

"But, I… what?"

He rounded the corner and ushered me into a large room. I reached for my iLs and panicked a little when I realized I'd left it in the car, along with my purse.

"Welcome," he said, holding out his arm.

There were about fifteen people, close to my age—give or take ten years—seated on couches, chairs, or the floor. Mitchell was among them, but he avoided eye contact with me as I glanced around the room. The rest of the men and women were looking straight at me. Some smiled; some showed no emotion at all. None of them said a word. I braced myself for their incoming thoughts, but nothing came.

The silence was overwhelming. My breath started coming faster as a sense of panic settled in. I'd never been without my iLs in a room filled with so many people without hearing a single voice in my head. After years of wishing for silence, it was surprisingly unsettling now that I had it. Deafening, even. *Maybe I've gone deaf.*

"You're not deaf," the gorgeous guy said.

"I... what?"

"Or maybe you are. You've been saying 'what' a lot lately."

A few people chuckled, and I looked at them as if they were aliens. What was happening here? Why couldn't I hear anyone? And what was the deal with this guy? Was he really reading my mind? Was it too much to hope there was someone else in this world like me?

"Oh, for God's sake. Put her out of her misery already, O. I can't listen to all these questions anymore," a blonde girl sitting Indian style on the floor called out.

She can't listen to all these questions...

"If she doesn't have a panic attack soon, I might have one just from listening to her," someone on the couch said.

"Mackenzie, maybe you should sit down." The gorgeous guy—O, apparently—gestured toward an open seat.

"I'm fine, thank you." My eyes darted from person to person, and then landed on Mitchell, silently pleading for answers, reassurance, anything. He looked away, obviously uncomfortable.

"Suit yourself," O said as he found himself a seat, leaving me the only one standing, in a room full of people staring silently at me.

"Welcome, Mackenzie. We are the Unseen."

9

"Unseen? More like unheard! Would someone please tell me what's going on? Mitchell? Come on, man." The panic was starting to eke into my voice. Mitchell shrugged his shoulders and shifted uncomfortably.

O didn't acknowledge my comment to Mitchell. "I'm trying, but you keep interrupting me."

"Pretty sure I interjected just the once."

"Do you want answers to your questions or not?"

I decided to push him. "What questions?"

He was unmoved. "Who we are, why you can't hear us, and if we're reading your mind." I blinked at him, so he continued. "Like I said, we are the Unseen. You can't hear us because we've learned to protect ourselves against other readers, and yes, we are reading your mind."

I put out a hand to steady myself, but I wasn't close to a chair or anything to grab onto, and I ended up sort of flouncing to the floor.

"Bet you wish you'd taken the chair now," O said. He met my glare with a smile.

Here I was, in a room full of people just like me. All this time, I had thought I was alone. A freak. But now I knew there were others who shared my ability.

Picking up on my thoughts, O bristled. "You are *not* a freak. None of us are."

"Stop." I put my head down on my knees and covered my ears, like that would keep my thoughts from escaping. "I can't think with all of you in my head." With each word, my voice raised another decibel.

"Okay, you're right. This is a lot to handle. Let's start over." He stuck out his hand. "Hi. My name is Owen, but everyone calls me O. I'll take you downstairs to meet the boss. He's the one with the authority to give you some answers. On our way, maybe you'd like to see the joint?"

I eyed him, completely unsure of what to do. I felt caught between two worlds, the one where I had direction and purpose, but no sense of belonging, and this new and scary one. I took a deep breath. *You came here to find out who this guy was. Now you know. And it's more than—*

"I'm gonna stop you right there. Let's leave a few things to the imagination, shall we?"

A crushing thought occurred to me. *He's heard everything. All my stupid, girlish thoughts.* My stomach rolled at the thought.

He chuckled. "You're not the first girl to fall for my devastatingly good looks."

"Your arrogance takes off a few points," I said aloud.

He laughed. It was a deep, rolling sound, but there was obvious joy in it too. He was someone who took great pleasure in laughing. "Indeed. Should we take that tour?"

"Why not?" I said, liking him a little more in spite of myself.

"Great." He didn't waste any time. "Well, this is the sitting room. It's where we all sort of gather to relax or watch movies and TV."

I nodded to a few people who were smiling encouragingly at me as we walked to a set of double doors across the room.

"Through here is the kitchen."

It was huge and state of the art. Stainless steel covered

every appliance, the countertops were granite, dark wood cabinets lined three of the walls, and an island divided the food prep area from the eating area. Two long tables with seating for about twenty helped me envision fun, noisy meals here. After spending so many meals alone, even when I was a kid, it was hard to imagine myself at the table.

"Yeah, it can get loud if we all eat at the same time. But it's rare for every seat to be full, if that helps."

I nodded, and he led me through a second set of double doors at the back of the kitchen. This room was smaller and narrower than the previous two. All four walls were lined with books. A small table with a lamp was at its center, and there were plush chairs scattered around.

"This is our library, obviously. There are a few here who like to read, and a few others who like to study and try to learn more about the science behind mind reading, things like that."

"Science behind mind reading? I thought the general belief was that mind reading is science fiction, not science," I said as I gazed up at the floor-to-ceiling shelves. There was everything from Dante's *Inferno* to *What Every Body is Saying* by some guy I'd never heard of. I had to stop myself from reaching for that title, wondering how much truth there was in it.

"That one's good. I wonder if he actually is a mind reader, to be able to read so much into body language and what people are communicating without actually saying."

I nodded, making a mental note to buy the book.

"You could just read it here."

I looked at him blankly. He expected me to come back, like over and over again. At least enough times to read a book.

"Right. Let's move on." He led me through another set of doors that opened to a room just as narrow as the library, but a little longer.

"This is our game room. Mostly the guys hang out in

here, but we have one or two gamer girls who like to join us."

They had everything—Ping-Pong, pool, and at the end of the room, a huge television with several of the latest gaming systems connected to it.

I whistled. "Man. You guys don't spare any expense here, do you? How do you afford all this?"

"Our benefactor is very generous." He held the next set of double doors open for me, which led us back to the sitting room. We'd made a giant square, as far as I could tell.

"Whatever that means."

Mitchell made eye contact with Owen from across the room, nodded, and got up to leave.

"What's his deal?" I asked, wanting to know more about my rescuer.

Owen didn't answer right away. I wasn't sure if he was hesitating because he didn't want to betray his friend's confidence, or if he truly didn't know. "Mitchell is complicated. His journey to the Unseen left him a bit broken. Someday, he might share his story with you. But it should come from him, not me or anyone else."

"You two must be close if you're privy to that information."

"Well, we're all friends, but yes, I suppose Mitchell and I are closer. He and I joined the Unseen around the same time a while ago. He's the closest thing to a brother I have left." We started walking back to the stairwell.

"He joined the Unseen before I did, but only by a few weeks. My road here was... rocky to say the least. Mitchell took me in, showed me the ropes, and really helped me feel at home. And it had been a long time since I'd felt that way anywhere." He looked wistfully in the direction his friend went, and I wondered just how deep his ties to the Unseen were.

I waited for him to elaborate, but he moved on. "At any rate, lucky for me, it turned out Mitchell is a pretty cool guy once he lets you get to know him. Just give him a chance."

I nodded, knowing I wouldn't get any more information on the subject, and I'd gotten what I wanted initially anyway, so I changed the subject a little. "Where are we going now?"

"To finish the tour." I followed his gesture and realized the stairwell didn't end at this floor, like I'd assumed it did. He led me down another flight. This one too was protected by a huge, metal door, but it had a keypad lock. Once he'd punched in the code, the heavy door creaked open and dumped us into a hallway.

"These are the dorms." He walked to the third doorway. "This one is mine"

He pushed inside, revealing a relatively large room with a double bed against two walls, a dresser next to the bed, and a small television on the back wall.

"You live here?" I surveyed the room. It was every bit as nice as my own room, except it didn't have any windows. They'd added plants and other natural textures to make it feel less confining, despite the lack of natural light.

"Yup." He paused, possibly debating his next words. "You could too, if you wanted."

"I could…" I paused. "Wait, what?" I could live there. *This could be a good option if I don't find a job before the end of the summer.* My heart began to race.

"Let's not get too far ahead of ourselves. There's a lot to consider before you decide whether you want to move in."

"What do you mean?" *A catch. I knew it.*

"Not so much a catch as a commitment."

"Commitment?" *What kind of commitment? Who exactly were these people? Is this a creepy cult or something?*

He laughed. "No. We're not a cult. Let's finish the tour, and maybe that will help answer some of your questions."

We walked back to the stairwell. "All the dorms are the same as far as furnishings go. But we decorate them however we want."

"Does everyone have their own room?"

"Yup."

"What about the fact that there aren't any windows? How would you get out in a fire? Aren't there laws against that?"

"I'm sure there are. Those who choose to live here accept the risks."

He didn't elaborate. *Risks?* I didn't care much for that word… or the fact that he'd used the plural form of it.

The next floor was guarded a little more heavily. Owen stood in front of an eye scanner, then when the light turned green, placed his thumb on a pad next to the door and it creaked open, just as the one above did.

The floor was organized into smaller rooms resembling offices. There were windows on all the doors, making it feel more open and inviting. Most of the rooms were empty, but there were a few people sitting at tables flipping through paperwork, working on computers, or listening to laptops or iPads with headphones.

"This is what we call the work floor. It's where the magic happens when we're not out on assignment."

"Out on assignment? What kind of work do you do?" *Maybe I could work with these people,* I thought. But what would they want with a music therapist?

He laughed. "We do mostly confidential stuff," he said. His debonair smile didn't do anything to quell my curiosity, but I decided to keep quiet for now. "As for our current openings, you can ask the boss when you see him. We always have room for more readers, though."

We came to the bottom floor, and he pushed open the door. It was a gym filled with an extensive array of equipment. Punching bags hung from the ceiling, machines and free weights lined the walls, and the open space off to one side was…

"That's for hand-to-hand training," Owen filled in for me.

"Hand-to-hand training? Like fighting?"

"A bit more elegant than that, but I suppose."

"So, karate?"

"Not quite that elegant."

"I see," I said, even though I didn't see at all. Who on Earth were these people?

He led me toward three sets of doors along the back wall. "The first two rooms are for individual training."

"Individual training, like what?" I peeked through the tall, skinny window in one of the doors. The room was small, with two chairs, a white board, and a television. It reminded me of a practice room at FSU, without the piano.

"Oh, like learning to guard your mind."

I had never dreamed of doing something like that; until now, there had been no need. "Is that something I could learn to do?"

"Absolutely. You'll learn that and more if you join us." He smiled slyly at me. "That way, we can all get a little peace."

I shoved him, and he laughed that beautiful laugh of his. When he stopped, I wanted to say something funny just to hear it again.

He cleared his throat, and I realized he'd probably picked up on my thoughts. If he did, he was kind enough not to draw too much attention to it. "And here we are at the end of our tour." We stood in front of the last door in the back corner of the gym. It looked just like the other doors, so I assumed it led to another training room.

"This is the boss' office. Normally, he doesn't see people on their first day, since not everyone decides to stay. But he asked to see you."

"What? Why?"

"Who knows? Maybe he could hear your incessant and scattered questions and wanted to silence them."

"Silence them like how? Kill me and stuff me in some creepy drawer four floors underground?"

He laughed. "I think you watch too many serial killer movies. You don't have anything to worry about. You're safe here."

I spied some of the heavy equipment on the other side of the room and raised my eyebrow skeptically.

"You are. Anyway, he knows you're here and he's waiting to see you."

I hesitated, knowing Maddie would not approve of any of this. In fact, she was probably going nuts since I'd ignored her texts for the last hour or two. I glanced at my watch. It was already 2:30, so she was probably most of the way home by now.

"He will only take as much time as you want to give him."

"You make it sound like it's his privilege to see me, not the other way around."

He shrugged. "I'll be waiting out here to take you topside when you're done."

Something puzzled me. "Why are you the one guiding me through this?"

"You better go in," he said, ignoring the question.

"There may come a time when you won't have an unfair advantage over me. Then what will you do?"

His eyes danced with merriment. "Enjoy the challenge."

"We'll see," I said, and turned to go into the boss' office.

I raised my hand to knock on the door, but he called out, "Come in," before I could make contact.

"Hello Mackenzie. I've been waiting a long time for you." He sat behind a cherry wood executive-style desk with bookshelves behind him filled with books on every possible subject, everything from *All the King's Men* to something called *The 33 Strategies of War*.

He let me linger a bit, allowing me to take in the room and my surroundings before gesturing to the chair across from his desk. "Please, have a seat."

After easing myself into the surprisingly comfortable chair, I looked him over. He looked middle aged, and was by far the oldest person I'd seen in the place, with salt-and-pepper hair, glasses, and a huge mustache that hung down over his top lip. I wondered how he kept it clean, but of course, I didn't ask. Instead, I said, "So, how come you've been waiting so long for me?" After what Owen had told me, I had the impression I was special in some way, but I couldn't put my finger on how.

He chuckled. "I try not to eat anything terribly messy, but it generally cleans up pretty well. Don't hesitate to tell me if something is caught in it though. Wouldn't want to look foolish." I laughed, and he continued before I could comment. "You are special, but you need to discover the reason for yourself."

"Is that the name of the game here? Aloof answers to direct questions?"

"Depends on the question, I suppose. What else do you want to know?"

"Got any job openings for a music therapist?"

He smiled. "No, but I do have an opening for you if you're interested."

"What are the pay and benefits like?"

"Excellent."

I eyed him, feeling like I was missing something important. "A short answer."

"I can go into details once you agree to work here."

That seemed fair to me. Not all employers would be free with information, particularly where it came to confidentiality of patients, duties, and possibly methods.

"And what exactly would my job responsibilities be?"

He sat back in his chair. "Each assignment is different and all are highly confidential."

"Okay, well, give me a for instance. I'm having trouble

picturing what mind readers do for a living."

"We read minds, Mackenzie."

I frowned, getting frustrated, but before I could ask another question, he held up his hands. "Fine. For example, in the beginning, you might be asked to provide background information on a mark for an assignment. As you advance with us, your tasks will involve more and more reading."

"Background information? So you target certain people for readings? To what end?"

"To all different ends. It depends on the assignment."

"Also, I'm not a researcher. I'm a music therapist. How do you know I would be any good at this job?"

"Let's just call it a gut feeling."

His evasive answers were making me uneasy. Clearly picking up on my thoughts, he said, "Listen, as with any job, I'll be able to provide you with more details once you commit. The work is classified, so for now, this is all I can give you." He looked like he meant it—that he'd like to give me more information but couldn't—so I decided to let it go for now.

"Fine, but I have one question that has nothing to do with me working here. It's pretty clear that Owen and Mitchell followed me. Why?"

He frowned. "I hope you don't see that as a breach of privacy. Mitchell wasn't following you initially. He stumbled upon you in your time of need, and then he reported to me that he'd found a reader who had no idea other readers existed. He felt your need to belong, all your questions about who and what you were. So I sent Owen to confirm his suspicions. When he did, I gave him the go ahead to make contact."

Finally, a straight and truthful answer, from what I could tell. It gave me the confidence to go back to asking him questions about my potential future with the Unseen. "Owen said I could live here if I wanted, and he implied it would be rent free. But he also said it would require a commitment of sorts. What exactly does that mean? Is room and board one of the benefits?"

"Owen is right, our members live on site, and I suppose it is part of the benefits package. If you want to be one of us, you must live here, and make a full-time commitment to honing your gift."

"My…" I hesitated. "Gift?"

"That's right."

I'd never thought of it that way. It had always been more of a curse—a burden, at best.

The boss frowned. "I am sorry you've been alone for this long. Normally, we would have tried to approach you sooner. Circumstances kept us apart. But I do hope you'll consider staying. Just imagine your potential, Mackenzie, how different your life could be if you knew how to control your gift."

Control it, I thought, tempted by the possibility. I shook my head, struggling to bring rational thought back to the forefront. "Although I'm excited about this new opportunity, I just graduated from grad school, and I have a lot of applications out there. I've spent the last six years pointing myself down the road I'm on. I'm not sure I want to change direction so suddenly."

"Music therapy is important to you, isn't it?"

"Yes. It's been my dream ever since I found out about it. I need to help people. I need to be surrounded by music." I paused, trying to picture myself living there. "Come to think of it, there's nowhere really for me to play, if I did move in here."

"We would find a way to accommodate your recreational playing. But if you decide to work here, it would mean giving up a career in music therapy."

Hearing it out loud made me cringe. It didn't feel right. "Sell it to me. I'm not sure you understand what you're asking me, and I deserve a thorough explanation before making such a tough decision."

"That's fair. Learning to master your gift will take all

of your energy and focus. This place is rent free, and all your expenses will be covered when you live here, but there's no such thing as a free lunch, and dedicating yourself to the process is the price you would pay to be here."

"All my expenses would be covered? What exactly does that mean?" I asked.

"If you need something, ask and it will be provided."

His ask-and-ye-shall-receive answer was a little unbelievable and creepy too. Where did all of the money come from? I was quiet for a moment, and then I said, "Not to be greedy, but is there a salary on top of this all-expenses-paid gig, or is it just a blank check kind of deal?"

"I suppose technically there is no salary. As I said, if you need something, you will have it."

I sat back in my chair, unsure if a legitimate business could actually run like that. "It sounds too good to be true, until I think about the sacrifices you're asking me to make… particularly since I have so little to go on."

"I'm sorry to be the one to make you choose."

I shook my head, tears suddenly threatening. I felt like I had come close to finally understanding who I was, and now it was being snatched away from me. "I don't understand why everyone is always trying to come between me and my dream. It seems like my friend Maddie and the professors at FSU are the only ones who believe in me."

He looked at me with a lot more sympathy than I would have expected to get from a total stranger, almost like his heart was breaking for me. "I'm sorry to put you in such a difficult position. Unfortunately, life is a series of difficult choices— which school to attend, which man to marry, whether or not to have kids, then how many kids to have, where to raise them, where to send them to school. All of these decisions have the power to alter the course of your life. As in this case, neither choice is necessarily right or wrong. But it is one you will have to live with for the rest of your days. It shouldn't be taken lightly."

I felt like he'd just laid a hundred tons of bricks on me. "First of all, I just met you. I'm not sure I need a lecture on life lessons."

I looked deep into his steel eyes, demanding an actual answer to my next question. "How can I choose between something I've been reaching for my whole life and something so unlikely I never even dared to hope for it?"

"Only you can decide which path your feet should follow."

Um, okay, Rafiki.

He seemed confused by my thought, but he didn't press me. "Why don't you think about everything and come back another time?"

Taking that as my cue to leave, I stood, disappointed that this opportunity to gather information about the Unseen had ended, but relieved to be free of the pressure to make an immediate decision.

"Fine," I said. "Nice to meet you?" I phrased it more like a question, not really sure what was socially acceptable to say to the leader of a group of mind readers.

"It was an absolute pleasure to finally meet you, Mackenzie." He smiled, like he meant it more than I did. A lot more than I did. "I do hope to see you again soon."

My only response was to nod and walk out of his office.

Owen was waiting for me.

"How'd it go?" he asked.

"Could've been better. I'm sure it could've been worse, but I can't imagine how at the moment."

We were alone in the gym, and his voice echoed a little when he asked, "Do you want to talk about it?"

I looked at him, not ready to open up to this person I'd just met... even though I wished I could. Somehow, I knew he would understand in a way Maddie never would.

Alarm flashed across his face. "You can't talk to your friend Maddie about what happened today."

"Well, I certainly won't tell her I spent the day with a group of mind readers who want me to join their cult, if that's what you're worried about." The tears in my throat made my voice thick. "She doesn't know what I am, anyway."

He shook his head. "Please don't say anything. It's not just for your own safety, it's for hers."

"Safety? But you said I wasn't in any danger here."

"No. In fact, you're probably safer here than you are out there."

"What is that supposed to mean?"

"You know what? Nothing. It doesn't mean anything. Just forget it. But please keep this to yourself. It's a decision you need to make without Maddie's input."

That made me bristle. It felt like an exclusive club where you were either in all the way, or you were out. "What is this, the Free Masons or something? You know, all these secrets are just exhausting. How am I ever supposed to make this kind of decision without all the facts? Your boss in there just gave me a lecture about making hard choices, but he didn't even tell me his name. I've known other mind readers exist for all of a few hours, and I'm suddenly supposed to turn my life upside down for you? Potentially cut friends out of my life who are like family to me? Talk about wham, bam, thank you ma'am."

"You're right. It's a decision none of us took lightly." He paused. "Although, I suppose that isn't really true. I sort of dove in headfirst, but that's neither here nor there. This is about you, not me."

"And are you happy with your headfirst dive?" I watched him carefully, trying to decide if he would tell me the truth or not. Without being able to read him, I supposed I'd never know for sure.

He looked me straight in the eyes, making me shiver. "I'm getting happier with it all the time."

We didn't speak while he walked me back to my car, and I

tried hard to clear my thoughts so he couldn't hear them. I focused on breathing in and out slowly. In. Out.

When we got to the car, I turned toward him, but I didn't make eye contact. I wasn't sure what to say, so I was glad when he spoke first.

"Mackenzie, I do hope I'll see you again." He held my hands in his and looked steadily into my eyes, but he said nothing more.

I simply stared back at him, losing myself in eyes that were almost too dark for me to tell where the pupil ended and the iris began. I needed to be careful, or I'd never walk away from him.

Just breathe. I released him and got into my car, thinking of nothing but breathing. In. Out.

10

The shaking didn't set in until I parked in my driveway. Still sitting in my car, I pulled my phone out of my bag and it flopped around about like a fish out of water until I got a handle on it. I had four messages from Maddie.

So bored! Where are you? You should be home by now!

The guy next to me is a total mouth breather, and he's stinking up the whole car.

One more hour and a few more papers to grade!

So... trying hard not to worry that you're lying in the middle of the street after some horrible car accident or something. Call me, ok?

She picked up on the first ring. "You're alive!"

"Yes! Sorry. Something came up." *Please don't ask any questions about it. Please don't ask any questions. Please...*

"Like what?"

Damn it. "Just an opportunity. I need to look into it a little more before I make any decisions."

"An opportunity? Like a job opportunity? That's great! Why didn't you say something about it yesterday? Maybe you don't recall this giant conversation we had about your job prospects? That would have been a perfect opportunity to mention it!"

"It came up kind of suddenly, like on my way home from dropping you off suddenly."

"Wow! So, tell me about it. What's the job? Is the pay good? When would you start if they hire you?"

Well, truth be told, I was with a bunch of mind readers who want to train me to be a better reader, and if I accept, I have to give up my dream and go live with them. Exit Maddie stage left. "Basically the job is mine if I want it. Pay is livable, but there are some major drawbacks to consider."

"Like what?"

"Well, I can't go into too many details, which frankly is one of the drawbacks."

"What does that mean? You're supposed to keep it a secret?"

I didn't say anything.

"Whoa, did you get tapped by the CIA or something? That would be so cool!"

I smiled. Nope, no judgment here. Just shining, unconditional support. I wondered what she would say if she knew the truth, all of it. "Um, not exactly. All I can say is it would mean giving up any involvement in music therapy. That's the other major drawback. Oh, and I have to live on campus."

"What do you mean—you'd have to give up music therapy? You've dedicated your whole life to it. How can you even consider this opportunity?"

I paused. How could I convince her without telling an outright lie? It was a constant source of guilt for me that she never kept secrets from me, and I'd been keeping a huge one from her for our entire relationship. I'd thought of telling her the truth many times, of course. In my best-case scenario, she'd be understanding—she'd think my talents were super-hero cool and she'd want to know more about them. But our world was far from perfect. As amazing as Maddie was, telling someone you could read minds was bizarre at best, crazy talk at worst. In the end, I was never willing to risk our friendship in the selfish interest of unburdening myself of the secret.

"Let's just say it's something I never even knew I could hope for."

She was silent while she waited for me to provide details that I couldn't give her.

"Okay, well, I don't really know what that means. I do know you, though, and I know you wouldn't think about abandoning music therapy lightly, so this must be important. I know you'll do the right thing."

Blown away. That was how I felt. She wasn't mad I was keeping secrets, demanding more details, or judging me for thinking of throwing away the last six years of hard work. I marveled at how she could still surprise me after decades of friendship.

"Thank you." It seemed an insufficient thing to say, but it was the only thing that came to mind.

"What do you think you'll do?"

It was the million-dollar question. "Honestly? I have no idea."

I spent two days stewing about the Unseen. By Tuesday, I was no closer to a decision. Letting Mitchell walk out of my life without getting any answers from him had been one of the biggest regrets of my life. How could I let something like that—yet on a much larger scale—happen again? How could I resist the chance to surround myself with people just like me, people who could teach me how to better myself? On the other hand, how could I abandon my life's work, turning my back on the grants and scholarships that had been given to me in good faith? More importantly, how could I give up something that had been my passion for nearly twenty years?

I was chewing a piece of biscotti to a pulp, as if that would bring me answers, when a knock on the door jerked me out of my thoughts. Swallowing, I rose to answer it.

Peering through the peephole, my breath caught in my chest. *Owen.*

"The one and only," he said through the door.

I hesitated in opening the door. "What are you doing here? And how do you know where I live?" I called out. My eyes grazed the apartment, taking note of the dirty dishes on the coffee table, the half-folded load of laundry on the couch, and a halfheartedly read newspaper strewn across the floor.

"I wanted to see you today. And I have my ways of getting information."

I groaned inwardly.

"I suppose I can come back if you're not feeling up to company."

The tug of being with another reader—and not just any reader, but Owen—was becoming familiar, and it drove me to open the door. He greeted me with a smile, wearing basically the same outfit, jeans and a T-shirt, despite the fact that it was getting warmer every day.

"Why are you here?" *Sure, cut to the quick. Don't offer him a friendly greeting that might actually make him like you. Also, he's probably listening to this, you idiot.*

He smirked.

"Want to go for a walk?"

"It's getting kinda warm out for a walk, isn't it?" In truth, I'd walk just about anywhere with him, but I wanted to know his intentions first. I was sick of being caught off guard.

"I'm more comfortable when my feet are busy."

"Shockingly, I didn't have your comfort in mind when planning my day."

He stared at me, and I stared right back. Folding my arms across my chest, I tried to wait him out, but his beautiful brown eyes pleaded with me, so I relented, even though I hated myself a little for doing it.

"Fine. Just let me grab my keys. Do I need my wallet?"

No, he thought.

It startled me so much I nearly tripped on my way to

get my keys. No one had ever deliberately communicated with me through their thoughts before. "How did you...?" I trailed off, not sure how to even finish my thought.

You could do it too, if you wanted.

I snapped myself out of the awed trance I was in, forcing myself to keep moving toward the door, where Owen waited for me. "How useful could something like that be? Unless I was around other readers and we didn't feel like talking. Or hey, maybe if we all came down with some particularly nasty laryngitis. In day-to-day life, though? Not super helpful."

"You never know when something like that can save your life or someone else's."

"What? You're verging into creepy territory again," I said, turning to lock the door behind me. "Why would I be in danger? And I can't really envision a scenario that would require me to get into another reader's head."

"You're thinking about this particular skill all wrong," he said as we walked down the sidewalk, cars whizzing past, ruining any hope of a peaceful walk. "I'm not inserting myself into your mind. I'm selectively allowing you into mine."

"So you can... choose what I hear?"

"Yes, a slight perfection on the protection techniques you could learn." He paused, looking down at his feet as he walked, hands jammed in his pockets. I didn't need to read his mind to pick up on his inner turmoil. "If you decided to stay with us."

I had to admit the idea was intriguing. But something still made me hold back. "I just can't make that kind of commitment without knowing everything that's involved. I think any normal person would feel the same way."

"I suppose I'm not a normal person then," he said, an edge to his voice.

"You expect me to believe that you just blindly put your fate into the hands of complete strangers?"

"Yes."

I waited for him to elaborate, but he didn't. He just kept walking, eyes trained straight ahead on something I didn't see, mind totally closed to me. Finally, he looked over at a hobby shop we were walking past.

"There was one of these in the town where I grew up."

The comment totally caught me off guard, and I almost stumbled.

"I used to beg my mom to take me there every weekend, so I could get a new model car to build." He smiled, obviously fond of the memory. "But she always made me wait until I had enough money saved to actually pay for it. That just made it all the better when I actually got to go in and pick something out." He laughed. "They were having a sale this one time, and my mom had clipped a buy-one-get-one-free coupon so I got two. It was like Christmas."

"I didn't know you liked to build model cars."

He nodded and walked on, staring at his feet.

Part of me wanted to stay in this moment with Owen. It felt special somehow, this glimpse of his life *before*. But another part of me yearned to know what lay before me. And I knew Owen could tell me.

"And how did it feel to isolate yourself from your mom for the Unseen?"

"I didn't. She was already gone when I joined."

Gone, I thought. *What does that mean?* He didn't elaborate.

I threw up my hands, frustration taking over. I was tired of getting so close to real answers, then having the door slammed in my face. "Okay, this is ridiculous. You guys expect me to make some lifelong commitment without all the facts? Forget it. Go back home. I'm through. My career is worth more to me than this." I did an about face and headed back toward my apartment, leaving him standing alone on the sidewalk. I imagined what his face would look like, totally crushed by my rejection, and I reveled in that image a little.

"Wait just a second." He jogged to catch up with me, but I didn't slow my pace or turn to look at him. He reached for my arm to stop me. "Mac, seriously. You can't just walk away."

"Watch me," I said as I jerked my arm from him. "I'm sick of your secrets. It isn't fair. You know all of mine, yet you keep everything from me—secrets about reading, secrets about the Unseen, even secrets about you. If you want me to be in, I need to know what 'in' means."

"I understand where you're coming from. But that's not how it works. Listen, David sent me today to find out if you'll come back to our headquarters. That's kind of a big deal."

"Wait, who's David?"

"The boss."

"Why does he care so much if I come back?"

"Not sure. But he does. Think of it this way, just because you come back, doesn't mean you have to stay." He paused, pleading with his giant puppy dog eyes.

"Oh, for God's sake." I pointed at him. "You're using your powers for evil. Fine. But I'm only coming back on a fact-finding mission. If I don't get the answers I need to make an intelligent, well-informed decision, I'm done."

He swallowed, and I hoped it was because my confident and confrontational manner was making him nervous. He smiled, but only slightly. "Fair enough." After a few more steps, he looked over at me and said, "Mac, I hope you get the answers you need. I'd hate to have to say goodbye to you."

Before my girlish mind went into a complete tailspin, I called *Gaspard de la Nuit* to mind. Shutting my eyes, I let it consume my thoughts, allowing my feet to land where they may as we walked along the city street.

"That's a beautiful piece," he said quietly.

"Yes. It is." I kept my answer short, not wanting to

let him into my world, not when I still knew so little of his.

"What is it?"

"It's called *Gaspard de la Nuit.*"

"Gasbag de la noot?"

"Gasp—never mind. It's my Everest."

He was silent as we worked our way back to my apartment. I wondered if he had an Everest.

"Someday, I'd like to dive the Great Barrier Reef," he said.

"You scuba dive?"

"Sometimes. I suppose the reef is my Everest."

I smiled to myself, having learned something tangible about him.

When we got to my door, he gently reached for my hand. "Will you really come back?"

I looked at him, and the mixed messages he was sending threatened to put me over the edge. He seemed eager to get to know me better, to keep me around, but he kept shutting me out. "You know, for someone who says he'd hate to say goodbye to me, you're sure not giving me much to say hello to."

He dropped my hand, adding more bricks to the wall between us. *Wrong move,* I thought, but he ignored it.

"You need to understand…"

"That's what I've been trying to do since the day I met Mitchell."

"What?"

"Understand."

I thought I saw some sympathy in his eyes, but instead of responding directly, he said, "You'll have to tell me that story someday."

I couldn't keep up with the change of gears. "What?"

"How you and Mitchell met. He won't tell me."

"I thought I was an open book."

"You are. But I'd still like to hear it from you."

You build the wall up, and then try to reach out to me from the other side?

This is how it has to be. For now.

We stood in front of my door. I was so consumed by our conversation, it didn't occur to me to invite him inside. "For now? You mean I'll have the answers I seek once I commit? Once I effectively sell my soul to the devil?"

"Not exactly."

"Which part?"

"We're not the devil, Mac."

"Says who? Lots of people believe mind reading is witchcraft, devilry."

"Well, that makes you one of the damned right along with us."

I opened my mouth, but for the first time, I didn't have a reply. He had me.

He smiled triumphantly, deciding to take his winnings and run. "I hope I'll see you again soon."

"Well, if you don't, you seem to know where to find me."

"Indeed, I do." The charm oozing off him made me want to shiver, but I kept *Gaspard* safely in my mind as I turned to unlock the door.

"Well, nice seeing you again," I said awkwardly.

"Yes. You too, Mackenzie."

My full name sounded nice on his lips. He smiled, knowing he'd gained another point with me.

Exasperated, I sighed. "Goodbye, Owen." I turned and closed the door on his triumph.

"Bye, Mac," he said from the other side of the door. I watched him walk away through the peephole, and once I knew he was truly gone, I threw myself face-first into a pile of laundry and screamed, letting the bottled-up energy and feelings explode into the clean clothes. They could handle it better than I could anyway.

11

The next day, I resolved to go back to the Unseen and get some answers, but a phone call stopped me in my tracks.

Normally, I didn't answer unfamiliar numbers, but I changed my habits when my job hunt began.

"This is Mackenzie."

"Ms. Day? Hello. My name is Shelly Goldstein. I got your resume from Marcia Peterson. I was wondering if you'd have time to come in for an interview."

"Sure! Yes! What's the job?"

She laughed. "Yes, I suppose that is pertinent information. I own my own psychology practice. I have no training in music therapy, and I would like to be able to offer it to my clients. I think the advances in that field are very exciting, and Marcia said you were the one to call."

It was a little jarring to hear Professor Peterson called Marcia, but I was very flattered. "It sounds ideal."

"Well, thank you. We can discuss all the details of the position's pay, benefits, and work hours at your interview."

"When would you like me to come in?"

"When are you available? I have an open appointment tomorrow at one."

"Perfect! I'll be there."

"Okay, the address is 511 West Virginia Street. See you there at one."

"Wonderful. Thank you so much."

Completely dazed, I hung up the phone. This was the exact opportunity I had been hoping for, at least until I met the Unseen.

The clock always seemed to move so much slower when Maddie was at work, and I had something to tell her. At 2:15, I couldn't wait any longer. I knew she'd still be at school, but the kids left at 2:00 and I needed to tell her about my interview.

"Hey, Mac! What's up?" I knew she'd pick up on the first ring, but a small part of me was still relieved to hear her voice. She would help. She always did.

"Hey, so... guess what?"

"You took the new job and it's the most amazing and best decision you ever made, except for making friends with me."

"Not quite."

"Well! What is it?"

"I've landed an interview with a private firm interested in expanding to music therapy."

Silence.

"Are you still there?"

"Yeah, I'm here. What the hell are you going to do?"

"I was hoping you might offer some insight on the matter."

"Good God, Mac. I don't know. I will tell you one thing though. It could be worse."

"How on Earth could it be worse?"

"You could be facing the imminent end of your grant money with no job offers or prospects."

"You're right. If I'm going to have problems, these are the kind of problems to have." I sighed. "I'm just afraid if I make the wrong decision, it could shape my whole life."

"Mac, wrong decisions don't shape your life. Right ones do. Wrong decisions simply change the way you get to the right shape."

"But if I take the other opportunity, and it turns out to be the wrong choice, this music therapy job probably won't still be available." My mind was on a downward spiral.

"You're going to plan your life on probably? That's weak, Mac, and you're stronger than that."

"You know what I mean."

"And you know what I mean. If it's meant to be, it will be. Did you apply for an opening with the firm? How did they get your information?"

"No, apparently Professor Peterson gave the psychologist my information and said I was the person to call."

"Hmm. Sounds to me like the job is yours if you want it."

"Hence my problem."

"Do you want it?"

"Absolutely!"

"Do you want it at the expense of the other opportunity?"

"I don't know. It would mean never…" I hesitated, biting my tongue to stop myself from blurting out what I wanted to say—it would mean never getting answers. "It would mean I would never get to find out for sure if I made the right decision."

"That will happen no matter what you do. You can't walk two paths before committing to the one that's right. That's not how it works. You could always do what Robert Frost did."

I paused, trying to follow her train of thought. Being best friends with a Literature buff made it hard to keep up sometimes.

"Take the road less traveled."

"Which is?"

"You're the one standing in front of the 'two paths diverged in a yellow wood.' You tell me!"

I didn't have an answer. The paths before me appeared equally treacherous and enticing.

Maddie filled the silence. "At any rate, I don't think either decision is necessarily wrong. Even if you do take this other opportunity that doesn't have anything to do with music therapy, you'll still have the last six years of training. This decision won't make that disappear. If you change your mind, you can always go work at a school or in a hospital program if the opportunity with the firm is gone. That was your plan anyway, to work your way up."

"Sounds like you think I should pursue the music therapy job."

"I'm not trying to push you either way. I mean, I don't think you can go wrong with the music therapy job. It's been your dream forever. If you do take it, I think you'll be very happy. What more could you want?"

Answers. Others like me. Freedom. "Right. What more could I want?" I murmured.

"Right," she said, her tone unreadable. Sometimes when we talked on the phone, I was glad I couldn't read her, but not this time. I wanted to know what she really thought, so I could decide what to do.

Anger bubbled up at Owen and the Unseen. "I wish the other opportunity had never come along. I had everything planned out so perfectly until this happened."

"Oh, my lovely." I could tell she was shaking her head when she said it. "And there's your fatal flaw. Life loves to take your perfect plans and dump a bucket of paint on them. It's your choice to call it garbage or make something beautiful of it."

"Yes. You're right."

"Of course I am. Don't you know me at all?"

I laughed. "Yes. I forgot myself for a moment."

"Don't let it happen again." She eased the tension,

but only momentarily. "So, whatcha gonna do?"

Every time she said that to me, I always started singing the COPS theme song in my head. "Well, I'm gonna do the interview, that's for sure. Then I'll make a decision, I suppose."

"Assume the music therapy gig offers you tons of money, a great benefits package, and is everything you ever wanted, then what will you do?"

"I'll still wonder about the other job."

"Hmm."

"Indeed."

"Well, I think—" she cut herself off, censoring her response. "I think I'd better get some work done so I can get home. Only two days left with the kids, baby!"

"Bring on the summer debauchery!"

"Get ready!"

"Oh, I am." I smiled, picturing all the fun we'd have this summer if I weren't part of some borderline cult that might try to keep me somewhat isolated from her.

"Say goodbye, Mac."

"Goodbye, Mac."

"Smartie pants. Call me after the interview tomorrow, okay? What time was it?"

"One."

"Okay, good luck!"

"Thanks, I'm gonna need it."

"No, you're not. You're gonna totally nail the interview!"

"That's not what I'll need the luck for."

"Oh. Right. Yeah, good luck with that too," she said in a better-ye-than-me tone.

"Ha, thanks. All right, I'll talk to you later. Thanks for being amazing, as always."

"I can't help the way I am."

I laughed. "Bye," I said and hung up. Although the conversation was over, her words stayed with me. She was right; life had just dumped a huge bucket of paint on my plans. So, what could I do with the resulting mess? Of course, I wanted to make something beautiful, who wouldn't? But how?

Ravel and my keyboard kept me company late into the night. I slept in the next day, getting up with just enough time to get ready for my interview and go.

The one decision I did make the previous night was to wear my iLs to the interview. I knew it would probably be just Dr. Goldstein and me, but I didn't want to know what she was thinking. If it was good, it would be that much harder to say no, and if it was bad, it would hurt my feelings and the knowledge that Professor Peterson had recommended me would be humiliating. So, iLs it was.

The office was actually within walking distance, but I drove anyway. It was getting warm out, and I didn't want the hard work I'd put in to make myself presentable to go to waste. But, if I did take a job there, it would be nice to walk to work in the cooler months.

I ended up driving past the address a few times, because it was set back behind some other buildings. Flustered, I tried to take some calming breaths before heading to the door. Despite getting turned around, I had still arrived five minutes early. *Nothing to stress about here.*

The reception area was decorated with a minimalist hand and a token potted plant sat perfectly in the corner, not a speck of dust on its leaves. The receptionist greeted me warmly and told me Dr. Goldstein would be out any minute, so I had a seat on the immaculately clean couch to wait. I pulled my phone out to distract myself, but I didn't get very far before Dr. Goldstein appeared.

"Ms. Day. Hello, I'm glad you could make it."

I stood and shook her hand. She had blonde hair cut short in a severe bob, with streaks of silver throughout. She was dressed smartly, with grey slacks, a light pink blouse, and steel-framed glasses perched high on her nose.

"Thank you so much for the opportunity," I said.

"Follow me to my office, and we'll get started."

The room was painted a calming light blue color, and a couch and two chairs were arranged on one side, while a desk and some bookshelves took up the other half of the room.

"Please, have a seat." She gestured toward the couch.

I sat down and, surprisingly, she sat on the couch with me. I'd expected her to sit in one of the chairs, keeping some distance between us, although I wasn't sure why. Perhaps because she was a psychologist, and they were always analyzing people from a distance? *Don't be judgmental,* I chided myself.

"I see you have an iLs."

"Professor Peterson didn't tell you?"

"No. She simply said you were highly qualified for the position."

I smiled awkwardly, second-guessing my choice to wear the iLs. "Yes, well, that's why I wanted to be a music therapist in the first place. I want to help people the way I was helped."

"How long have you had your iLs?"

"Since I was five."

"Wow, I thought successful music therapy weaned the subject off after a time."

"Technically, yes. However, I still consider my case a success, because even though I still use an iLs, I'm highly functional."

"I see."

Her tone was hard to read, but I pressed on. "I think with a music therapy program, you need to see the potential for success in every case, then work to achieve it."

She leaned back, getting a little more comfortable on the couch. "I think that applies to almost anything, don't you?"

I nodded. "Yes, I suppose it does."

"The program is obviously in its infancy, and it would be your responsibility to shape it, acquire resources, and find clientele."

My mind raced. *My program to shape.* It really was a dream come true. "Sounds ideal," were the only coherent words I could form at the moment.

She gave me a slight smile, showing her approval. "Can you tell me a bit about what your vision would be for the practice?"

"Well, I'd probably want to start out small, focusing on a few clients at a time. That would allow me to customize my treatment to meet their specific needs." I paused, thinking of the case studies from my thesis. "For example, if someone's more tactile, I might include some instruments in the therapy to make him or her feel more involved in the process. If a technophile teenage boy came to me, I'd get some mixing software to let him play around with. Anything to achieve a breakthrough."

I paused, my mind starting to move faster than my mouth with the possibilities. "They're developing new techniques all the time, so the opportunity to constantly evolve is very exciting."

Her smile stretched wider. "Right. Okay then. Let's talk money. Starting pay is fifty thousand, with full medical. Unfortunately, I don't have a dental package available yet, but I'm working on it. You could probably expect that in the coming year or two."

"Whoa." It slipped out.

"I know, but if you can hang with me, I promise it'll be a great place to work. Oh, and you start with two weeks paid vacation and get an additional week every five years you work here. We close the week of Christmas, so you don't need to use your vacation then."

"Honestly, I don't think it could get any better."

She beamed. "Wonderful! When can you start?"

My throat closed. Accepting would mean never going back to the Unseen. Never seeing Owen again. My throat closed a little more. I coughed, trying to clear it.

"Would you like some water?"

I nodded.

She went to a mini fridge behind her desk—brilliant, I thought, then wondered if I would have a mini fridge in my office—and came back with a wonderfully cold bottle of water.

Sucking it down, I frantically tried to come up with something to say that couldn't be interpreted as disrespectful, but would still afford me some time to think.

"Would it be possible to think about it for a day or two?"

Her face fell. "What? But I thought this was what you were looking for?"

"It is!" I said, scrambling to explain. "It's just that another opportunity has come up, so now I need to choose."

"I see." Her tone was flat, and I could almost see the wheels in her head turning. "Is there anything I can do to persuade you?"

"No, you've already made this an exceedingly difficult choice."

She crossed one leg over the other and sat up a little straighter, clearly satisfied with herself. "Wonderful. Take all the time you need. You're the only one I'm considering for the position at the moment, to be honest, and I do hope you'll take it."

I stood and shook her hand. "I will certainly give it serious consideration."

"I suppose I can't ask for more than that. I hope to hear from you soon," she said as she led me out of her office and to the door.

"It's ideal, Maddie. Good money, benefits, paid vacation, and they're closed the week of Christmas! The whole week!"

"Mac, you knew it would be ideal, and not because

of the money or benefits."

"No, I know. She said I would be responsible for shaping the program. Her words, not mine. Can you imagine? I'd have free reign to reach out to people and make a difference in a real way."

"You knew this wouldn't be an easy choice."

The excitement drained out of my voice a little. "She said I was the only candidate she was considering right now."

"So?"

"If I turn her down, I feel like I'm leaving her in the lurch."

"Get over yourself!" Maddie said. "You're not leaving her in the lurch. It's a business. She'll keep running it the best way she sees fit. You have to do what's best for you. Don't make a decision like this out of some bizarre perceived guilt toward some person you've only spent like fifteen minutes of your entire life with."

She certainly had a way of putting things into perspective. "Yeah, I suppose."

"When do you have to give her an answer?"

"She said to take all the time I need."

"Really? That's very generous. I wouldn't string her along though. Make your decision. Put us all out of our misery."

"Yes. You're right." I made a decision as I hung up the phone. I needed more information, and the only way I was going to get it was making a trip down to the Unseen.

12

I went to the Unseen first thing in the morning. *I'm going to make my decision today,* I thought as I got out of my car.

Owen was already leaning against the building when I walked up, and the sight of him made my knees weak. "Heard you coming."

"Great," I said, less than enthusiastic. "So you know why I'm here." It was a statement, not a question.

"Tell me about the job."

"You already know everything, don't you?"

"Yes, but I want to hear it from you."

While we walked down to the basement, I told him all about the interview and offer. By the time we got to the bottom, I was done.

"Sounds ideal," he said. I thought I detected a hint of sadness in his voice at the thought of my leaving, but maybe that was just what I wanted to hear. He looked into my eyes, and I felt like he was trying to see my soul. The sensation made me shiver. "So, what do you think you'll do?" He knew I didn't have an answer yet, but he was asking anyway. Sometimes, I did that too, hoping some new revelation would pop into the person's head. It never did, but that didn't stop me from trying, and it hadn't stopped Owen either.

"I think I'm going to try to get some answers from the boss man."

Just then, David emerged from his office. Owen straightened up a bit more, and I gave him a perplexed look, trying to understand why he would puff himself up for this man. Respect was the only answer that made sense. I followed David back to his office, giving Owen one last glance over my shoulder.

"Thank you for coming back," David said as he seated himself behind his desk. "I hear there's been a complication."

"You could say that."

"Do you want to tell me about it?"

"There isn't much to tell beyond what you must already know. I'm a fairly open book, right?"

He nodded, and silence ensued.

"Listen, I came back to try to get some information from you, to see if you can sweeten the deal, because I have to say, your competition is steep."

"Fair enough, Mackenzie, but I don't know what I can do to 'sweeten the deal.' I don't have much control over what I can and can't offer you. It's more of a take-it-or-leave-it kind of thing."

"That's fine, I guess. Let me tell you what I'm struggling with and maybe you can provide a solution. Sound good?"

"I'll try."

"First, I'm not wild about the idea of moving in here. I've lived alone for the last six years. And this feels too much like a commune. How do I know it's not some creepy Hotel California deal?"

He laughed. "It's not some creepy Hotel California deal. Although, if you do decide to join, it is a member-for-life kind of thing. I suppose it's similar in that way."

"Member for life? So, if I choose this, I can *never* go back to music. What if it doesn't work out? What if you and I don't get along? What if I don't get along with anyone? What if you can't train me, and I'm a big waste of time? Doesn't that ever happen?"

"No. The training process is rigorous, and relatively foolproof, although I have heard of problems once or twice. None in my division."

"And how were those problems resolved?"

"I believe the two parties separated as amicably as possible."

"Vague."

He didn't respond.

"Right. Well, I still don't want to live here, at least not right away. I have enough money to live in my apartment through the end of the summer, and I'd like to stay there at least until then."

He thought for a moment, and not for the first time, I was irritated I couldn't read him. "I suppose that's reasonable. Frankly, I'd prefer you stayed here where I can keep an eye on you, but if you insist, you may stay in your apartment for the rest of the summer. But you will be responsible for showing up on time for all of your training."

"No problem. I've been showing up on time for classes for the last six years." *All right. One point down.*

"What else?" he asked.

"I really would like some more information about who you guys are before I make this apparent lifelong commitment to you. I don't sleep with men on the first date, let alone marry them."

He cleared his throat, uncomfortable for some reason. "No, I don't suppose you do." He mumbled something that sounded like 'thank God' but I couldn't be sure. "Unfortunately, I hate to beat a dead horse here, but I can't tell you anymore. At least not until you've been here for a while. You will have to decide based on the information you have."

"And if I choose the therapy job?"

He frowned but nodded. "That's your right, and I'm quite sure you will be happy there."

Ha. I don't think that's what you really mean, I thought, not brave enough to say it out loud.

"No, it *is* what I mean. Obviously, I'll be disappointed if we don't get to work with you, but I'll be happy you're happy."

"Why? We just met. I barely know you. I didn't even know your name until Owen told it to me."

He leaned forward on his desk and looked me in the eye. "Mackenzie, it's like I told you before, you're special. That's very exciting. I hope to have the opportunity to see just how far you can go."

How far I can go? He didn't respond to my thoughts. He knew he'd just baited me, and he didn't want to jerk the hook out of my mouth.

"Was there anything else?"

I tried to collect my thoughts. "Um, yes. I think I know the answer, but I suppose it warrants asking. If I choose therapy, can I still come here? See Owen? Maybe train over the weekends or after work?"

He gave me a sympathetic look. "Mackenzie, you can't expect to succeed if you divide your focus that way. I'm sorry, but it's not possible."

I sighed and slumped back in the chair, not ready to face the world outside his office.

"You know what?" he said. "I'm going to take a walk. You can stay in here as long as you'd like." He stood and walked to the door, pausing before he left. "Mackenzie?"

I turned to see him waiting with his hand on the doorknob.

"Find me with your answer before you leave."

I nodded, and he left me alone with my future.

I wasn't sure how long I sat there. I kept thinking he would come back. He must have had work to do. But he left me alone, just like he'd promised.

Owen was waiting for me right where I'd left him. When I saw him, I wanted to run to him, put my arms around him, and let him make this decision easier for me. But I didn't. I couldn't. Instead, I took a deep breath, trying to clear some space in my head for rational thought, and crossed the gym, closing the distance between the two of us.

When I reached him, he was the one who folded me into his arms, and it felt more like home than anything I'd ever experienced. His smell, clean with a hint of men's deodorant, intoxicated me. He put a hand on my head and ran his fingers through my wild hair, letting me rest my head on his shoulder. No rush. No push to get away. He just held me.

The thought of never seeing him again hit me like a semi-truck, sucking the breath out of my lungs. If I walked away from the Unseen, Owen would be out of my life. Not only would I be losing the chance to discover who I really was, I'd also be losing the chance to share the experience with someone who truly understood.

Owen felt the change in me. "What's wrong?"

"Everything." I was being ridiculous. A lovesick teenager. I couldn't base life decisions on a stupid crush I had on a boy I barely knew. Unless… "Owen, you know how stupid I am over you."

A smile worked its way across half his mouth. "I've heard some rumors."

"Do you feel the same way about me?"

His eyes turned dark, and the half second he stayed silent stretched on for an eternity. *No.* That was all he had to say. All he had to do was crush my dream of having a partner who shared my strange ability, and I would move on. The therapy job would be good for me. It was what I'd always wanted.

No. Such a short word to do so much damage, but in the end, it would be all right. I didn't know him, and he didn't know me—despite the fact that he could hear my every thought.

No. I waited for him to say it.

Instead, he leaned in, kissing me deeply, and sensation eclipsed thought. His lips were soft and warm, his hands tangled in my hair, my own hands wrapped around his shoulders, holding on for dear life. He pulled back before I was ready, but would I have ever been ready?

"Does that answer your question?"

"I need to find David."

"Not quite what I wanted to hear after giving a girl some of my best moves, but okay. How come?"

"To tell him I'm in."

13

First things first, I thought when I got home that night. It was only about seven o'clock. Dr. Goldstein had written her cell number on the business card she'd given me. I dialed the numbers, holding on to the memory of that kiss, and of how wonderful it felt to be around other people like me, to strengthen my resolve. Meeting the Unseen had revealed to me just how lonely I'd been without them, and the thought of going back to that world in which my abilities alienated me from everyone around me was unacceptable. I pushed "call," feeling good about my decision.

"Mackenzie! Tell me something good," she said, making it even harder. I didn't want to be responsible for stealing the enthusiasm from her voice.

"Unfortunately—"

She cut me off. "No, don't say unfortunately! Come on, Mackenzie, don't make me beg."

"No, please don't beg. Believe me, this has been a hard decision, but the other opportunity is something I just can't pass up. If I don't at least try, I will always wonder."

She sighed, long and heavy. "All right, well, I can't

begrudge you that. But listen, if for some reason it doesn't work out, please call me right away. I'm sure I can find something for you, even if this spot has been taken."

Her kindness broke my heart a little more. "Thank you so much for this opportunity, and for everything, Dr. Goldstein. I do hope our paths will cross in the future."

"I'm counting on it, Mackenzie."

As soon as we hung up, I dialed Maddie.

"What did you decide?" she demanded without even saying hello.

"I took the other one."

"Oh my God!" she yelled. I pulled the phone away from my ear and could still hear her clearly. "I *knew* that's the one you would choose! I knew it! This is going to be so exciting for you! A whole new direction!"

"Yup." One syllable was all I could squeeze in.

"So, when do you start? Do you know what you'll be doing? Have you met any of the people you'll be working with?"

"I start first thing on Monday morning. It sounds like I'll mostly be training for a while. I've met a few people. One person in particular sparks my interest."

"Oh, really?" I could visualize one of her eyebrows rising up into that this-is-about-a-boy-isn't-it position.

"Yup."

"Well, give me more than one word on the subject. What's he like?"

"He's gorgeous, of course."

"Of course."

"Good sense of humor."

"I assumed."

"And not a bad kisser."

"*What?*" she exploded. "Okay, um, *what?* Start at the beginning."

"Well, I'm not sure how much I should even tell you. Except that right or wrong, he helped make my decision."

"How's that?"

"I couldn't imagine giving up the chance to see where this goes."

"Aw, my wittle Mac is falling in love," she teased.

"I don't know about all that. Feels more like a dumb teenage obsession."

"That's fine. Except you never really had one of those. When we were teenagers, you were more likely to date a guy once and punch him in the face than become enraptured with him. What's different about this guy?"

I can't read his every gross guy thought, and we might be able to have an actual relationship because of it. "I don't know. It just feels right."

She didn't respond, and I imagined her smiling on the other end of the phone.

"I do know that saying no to the therapy job was one of the hardest things I've ever done. I just hope it's worth it."

"Well, I'm happy for you. And proud. You made a hard decision—went outside of your comfort zone. I think it'll be good for you. I mean, you're getting kissed, so it's already a step in the right direction."

I laughed. "Priorities."

"I'm just sayin'."

It was after ten by the time we hung up, and I went to bed not long after. Though I was exhausted, my mind raced with thoughts about what might happen on Monday, how far I could go with my "gift," and, of course, Owen.

Although I couldn't read him, I knew his feelings for me ran deep. Our kiss was proof positive of that. I'd never had someone genuinely feel that way for me, and it was exhilarating and terrifying at the same time. I wondered how dating worked with the Unseen. Were any of them married? Did any of them have lives outside of the group? It didn't seem like it. Still, I hadn't really spent much time with any of them. Anything could be possible.

I lay in bed, letting my mind run rampant for a while before finally turning to look at the clock. 2:02 burned through the darkness at me. *This is going to be a long weekend.*

I pushed Owen from my mind, a Herculean task, and pushed the excitement of Monday away too, finally letting sleep claim me.

I was hoping Owen might pop over like he had on Tuesday, but he didn't. Being such a new member, I didn't feel it was my place to go spend the weekend with the Unseen, so I busied myself with normal weekend stuff. I cleaned the apartment, went shopping, got some groceries, saw a movie, and played *Gaspard* incessantly, anything to help pass the time.

I tried desperately not to obsess about Owen's absence. Of course, that worked about as well as dropping a rock in a lake and hoping it would float. By Sunday night, I'd worked myself into a tizzy—worrying about why he hadn't stopped over and whether I'd made the wrong choice.

I woke up Monday morning before my alarm, too wound up to register how little sleep I'd gotten. Unsure of what my training would involve, I opted to face the day in khaki pants and a nice blouse, packing yoga pants, sneakers, and a tank top in my backpack in case they actually expected me to use the gym.

I showed up promptly at eight. Owen was waiting outside for me, leaning against the building in what I was coming to think of as his habitual pose. The morning light cast an otherworldly glow on his olive skin that made my legs forget how to function.

He walked over with a big smile on his face. "I have something for you."

"Already?"

"It's your key to the building. Now I won't have to meet you out here anymore."

"Oh. Ha," I chided myself. "I stupidly thought you were doing that because you wanted to see me. Of course you had to let me in."

His expression turned serious, and he reached for my face, tracing my cheek with his thumb. "Of course I wanted to see you." He let his hand drop. "I just thought you'd want your own key, so you could come and go as you pleased. Go out on the town. You know."

We walked toward the door, and I bumped him with my hip. "Right. I'm such a wild child."

"So I hear."

He handed me the key, and it looked so ordinary. Then he gave me a small envelope. "Those are your codes for the other doors. Your prints and things have already been entered into the system. You have access to everything except the work floor. You'll get that once you've finished training."

I decided to ignore the fact that they were still keeping secrets and shook my head. "So, why didn't you come see me this weekend? Hot date with another woman?"

He laughed. "Absolutely." When I looked at him, my eyes wide with horror, he laughed even harder. "Not really! I thought you might want some space after all this, to let it sink in."

"Oh. How courteous of you," I said, a little flatter than I'd intended.

We walked down the steps together. "Okay, well, clearly that was a mistake. You can attend my public flogging after your training."

I softened and laughed. "I wouldn't miss it. What's on the agenda for today?"

"Today, you meet Tracy."

Turned out, Tracy was my no-nonsense instructor. She was petite, a few inches shorter than I was, with big, blue eyes and long, blonde hair. But her doll-like appearance belied her temperament. Her voice was deep for someone so small, and it was obvious she wouldn't tolerate tomfoolery of any kind. She commanded a certain amount of authority, and even though she looked much younger, her experience and mannerisms made me place her in her late forties.

Owen told me that she'd been with the Unseen for quite some time, but he hadn't elaborated beyond that, which didn't surprise me. More secrets.

"Mackenzie," she said when we met her in the gym. It was a statement, not a question. "I'm Tracy. I'll be your instructor." She led me away from Owen, to one of the small rooms at the back of the gym. I returned Owen's thumbs-up with an unsure smile before turning to follow her.

Once we were both seated in the room, at opposite ends of a small table, she said, "Do you have any questions before we begin?"

"Yes, actually. Something's been driving me crazy. Owen keeps making jokes about how relieved everyone is that I'm starting my training because they're sick of hearing all of my questions."

"What do you want to know?"

"Why don't they just block me?"

She sat back in her chair and thought for a moment before speaking. "An untrained reader's thoughts are much louder and more difficult to block out than a regular person's." She paused to make sure I was following, and I nodded.

"Because of this, your voice can be... distracting. Only someone who's highly skilled can block someone like you all the time. Most of us can block you part of the time, but we all hear tidbits now and then. Except for maybe David. He hears what he wants to hear. Make sense?"

"So you're saying that when I'm not low man on the totem pole anymore, I won't be able to block new people one hundred percent because of how loud they are?"

"Exactly. As you learn to hone your skills, you'll naturally start controlling your volume, making it easier for other readers to block you. Then, you'll learn to quiet your thoughts so much that others won't be able to hear them, even if they're trying. Picture yourself like a lighthouse. Before you met us, you were super bright, so that we could find you. Now, we're teaching you to use the dimmer switch to avoid attracting unwanted attention."

"Unwanted attention?"

"Yes." She didn't elaborate. "Is that all?"

It was far from all, but I had more than enough to chew on for the moment, so I nodded.

"Blocking is still a while off for you, I'm afraid. You're going to start off by learning to zero in on a single voice."

"Okay…" I trailed off, not exactly sure what that meant.

"I mean that when there are multiple people in the room, I will teach you to hear only one person's thoughts. I will show you how to choose who you hear and who you don't hear."

"You can do that?" I felt for my iLs in my purse. "Without this?" I showed it to her.

She frowned, disgusted. "That is a crutch only the weak-minded use. You will not be allowed to use it here, or ever again for that matter." She jumped to her feet, snatched it from me, placed it on the ground, and unceremoniously crushed it beneath the heel of her shoe. Then she returned to her seat as if nothing had happened.

I swallowed the rising panic. My lifeline to the outside world had just been destroyed. *I can always buy a new one if this doesn't work*, I thought, trying to reassure myself.

"No. You will not get a new one of these ridiculous Band-Aids. When I'm through with you, you won't need or want one ever again."

I swallowed, but my mouth had gone dry, so all that went down was a lump of air, which offered no comfort whatsoever.

A short knock came at the door, and then a man slipped inside the room, shutting the door behind him. "I've invited Camden to join us today," Tracy said. "He will be our second voice." She nodded at him, and he returned the gesture. He gave me a quick smile before he seated himself next to Tracy, across the table from me. I felt like it was two against one.

"I suppose it is," Tracy said. "We are going to allow you into our minds at the same time. Your purpose is to listen to Camden only. I will be able to tell when you have succeeded, so don't even think about lying to me if you haven't achieved your goal."

I shook my head rapidly. Did anyone ever lie to her? I couldn't imagine what must have happened to that poor soul.

"It wasn't pretty," she said with a sly smile. "Shall we?" she asked Camden.

"Wait," I choked. "How do I...?" I trailed off, not sure how to verbalize what she was expecting me to do.

"Discipline your mind."

I waited for her to say more, but I was met by silence.

"I could elaborate. I can discuss the semantics of it with you until I'm blue in the face, but it won't help. You need to experience it for yourself. When it comes down to it, you just need to discipline your mind. Nothing more, nothing less."

Right. Sure. Okay. Discipline my mind. That's easy. I mentally rolled my eyes.

"Why are you here?"

It was such an abrupt question, I stammered to answer it. "Well, I... I wanted to learn how to control it."

"It?"

"What you all refer to as the gift."

"And what do you call it?"

"My curse, I suppose."

"It's not a curse. Get that out of your head before we go any further. It may not be a gift, but it's certainly not a curse. I like to think of it as a responsibility. And that means we don't treat it haphazardly, wantonly going through life using crutches to control it. We must work hard to use it to the best of our abilities, constantly honing it so that we're at our best every day, so that we can hopefully use our talent to bring some good to this world."

"Oh." I hadn't really expected an epic monologue from her, and I didn't know how to respond. Truth was, I'd never looked at it that way.

"Now, are you ready to begin?"

I took a deep breath. "As ready as I'll ever be."

Camden started thinking first. His voice came to me smooth and low, very Barry White. *Welcome! How's it going so far?*

Well, I'll let you know in a—

Tracy interrupted us. *No small talk. Just work.*

I looked at her. *What are we supposed to talk about?*

You are not to engage me. You are to block me out entirely. Get to work.

I scowled at her, and she scowled right back. Shifting my gaze back to Camden, I waited for him to say something else, but he didn't. Neither did Tracy.

So, any tips on disciplining my mind? I asked him.

I think it's different for everyone. The way I found my center might not work for you. I think that's why she said you have to—

Do it yourself, Mackenzie. Quit asking him for ways to cheat, Tracy interrupted again.

Stung, I blurted out, "I wasn't trying to cheat. You said to talk about work!"

She tilted her head, and her expression softened a bit. "Okay, clearly, you're not getting what's happening here. Let me walk you through it. You and Camden will share a thought connection. I will interrupt, trying to provoke you any way I know how. My job is to be as distracting as possible. Yours is to ignore me, filter me out, and eventually not hear me at all."

Feeling dumb and chided, I hung my head a bit.

"Maybe it's a good time for lunch? I'm getting a little hungry myself, Trace," Camden ventured.

"What?" I looked around for a clock. "It can't be time for lunch already."

"It is, if you want it to be," Tracy said.

"But I haven't learned anything yet."

She chuckled. "Sure you have. You've learned who Camden and I are. That's enough for the morning. We'll revisit this in an hour." Her soft demeanor vanished. "Don't keep me waiting."

"Of course not," I said as I stood and scrambled out of the small room, grateful for even a momentary escape.

Owen was waiting for me when I practically fell out of the room. I straightened, trying not to look like a complete buffoon.

"How's it going?" he asked, although I was certain he already knew the answer.

"I suck. But Tracy gave me a break for lunch, so let's go get some food."

"Oh, come on," he said as we walked toward the stairs. "You don't suck. No one can do it on their first day."

"Really?"

"Well, I don't know. I'm not the authority on training. You'd have to ask Tracy for some hard facts. But I'm sure almost no one can do it on their first day." I jabbed him as we finished climbing the stairs to the main floor.

"And you? Did you do it on your first day?"

He smiled devilishly. "Honey, I never kiss and tell."

I rolled my eyes. "So no, in other words."

He shrugged his shoulders. "Nope. Took me about a month."

I withered at the thought of accomplishing nothing for a full month, but the flurry of activity in the kitchen quickly distracted me. People were at the fridge getting food, making sandwiches at the counter, taking chips and snacks from the pantry, and a few others were already eating at the tables.

It was still an adjustment to be around so many people without my iLs. The image of my broken lifeline flashed in my mind. How would I function if it took me a whole month to learn anything? I swallowed the rising panic, bringing myself back to the bustling kitchen.

"Jeez, how do you get what you need without getting in the way?"

"What do you mean by 'getting in the way'?" he asked as he reached around the girl standing in front of the fridge to grab a bottle of water. "Want one?"

I nodded. In the end, I stood off to the side while Owen made us a couple of sandwiches, grabbed a few handfuls of chips, and carried our plates to the table.

"Thanks," I said as he put my plate in front of me.

"I may not have learned to zero in on one voice on my first day, but I've always known how to make a mean ham sandwich."

I smiled in spite of my mood.

Tracy and Camden came in and got their food, but they didn't stay. I wondered if they were friends outside of torturing new people together.

Owen laughed out loud. "They're not torturing you. Don't let Camden hear you say that. He'd be destroyed, the old softie."

"Camden? Really? He's so…" I trailed off, trying to come up with a politically correct way to describe him.

"Big, black, and intimidating?" Owen filled in between bites of his own sandwich.

"A bit less eloquent than how I was going to put it, but yes."

"Don't let him fool you. Tracy, on the other hand, is genuinely a hard ass."

"I picked up on that all on my own."

"Ha! So, you *are* learning something!"

The fire in my eyes was hot enough to wilt the lettuce on his sandwich.

"Oh, come on. What did you expect on your first day?"

"I don't know. *Some* kind of success," I said as I picked the crust off my sandwich and jammed it into my mouth.

He lowered his voice. "I think you being here at all is a success, but that's just me." He looked into his water bottle as he took a drink instead of making eye contact. "Listen, the world can be a terrible place. I know you've seen it. But as mind readers, we have the potential to help fix it. Someone once said something about how the opportunity to change or save one life was worth a little sacrifice. But I think she was talking about her favorite boy band or something to do with music. It probably doesn't apply here."

I swatted at him. "Yes, well, I just hope I can live up to everyone's expectations."

Putting down his water, he leaned in toward me. "What exactly do you think we're expecting?"

"I don't know. It's got to be amazing though, given the way you practically begged, lied, and cheated to get me here."

"Okay, no one lied or cheated, and I think begged is a harsh word to describe any of our interactions."

I rolled my eyes. "Typical insecure man. I was being facetious."

"Well, I don't know what that means because I would never behave that way." He hid his grin behind his sandwich.

I threw a chip at him.

"Hey! Don't waste good chips!" He picked it up off the floor and ate it. I cringed. "Five-second rule." He rolled his eyes dramatically. "Girls and their cleanliness. Jeez."

I laughed. "What time is it, by the way? I don't want to keep Tracy waiting."

"None of us do." He glanced at his watch. "Yeah, let's go." He gathered the plates and put them in the dishwasher, leaving no trace that we'd been there at all. Considering how many people had been through the kitchen at lunch, it looked surprisingly clean.

Owen approved of my observation. "That's the idea. We all pitch in and clean up after ourselves. This place would be a sty if we didn't."

We walked back down to the gym in silence. I was too consumed by the prospect of more failure to make small talk.

When we got there, Owen tried to encourage me. "Don't think about it like that. You'll get it eventually, and when you do, it'll be awesome. Like your Everest."

I frowned. "I already have my Everest. And I still haven't conquered that. The last thing I need is another unreachable goal." Despairing, I turned to face him. "Maybe this was a mistake."

He took me by the shoulders. "This was not a mistake. Nothing with you in it is a mistake." He paused, letting that sink in. Then he shook me a little. "Now, tuck in your bottom lip and get to work. There's no room for self-pity here."

I straightened up. "Yes, sir!"

He smiled at me, but I couldn't quite bring a smile to my own face. The prospect of the long lesson before me was too daunting.

And, as it turned out, I was right to dread my next lesson. The afternoon dragged on, drenched in failure after failure. Tracy continued to berate, attack, and otherwise annoy me as I tried desperately—and unsuccessfully—to focus on Camden. Although the work wasn't physical, I was sweating from the effort by day's end.

I'd lost track of time when Tracy finally sat back in her chair. "I think that's enough for today. We'll pick back up here tomorrow."

I frowned. "Can I try one more time?"

"Honestly, Mackenzie, I don't think one more time is going to make a difference. You're not going to have your epiphany moment today. You're just not. Might as well come to terms with that right now." She looked over at Camden. "You ready to call it a day?"

He nodded.

"No," I said, too loudly for the small room. "One more chance. That's all I'm asking. I refuse to end the first day of this new life in defeat." I thought I saw a flash of sympathy pass over Tracy's eyes, but it was so brief that I couldn't be sure.

"Fine. You have ten minutes."

What makes you think this time will be different? Camden asked me.

Taking a deep breath, I concentrated on Camden's voice and my breathing. I closed my eyes, hoping it would help me shut Tracy out that much more. *I don't know. It probably won't.*

I thought I heard Tracy's voice say something, but it was too quiet to make out the words. Not like a whisper, though, more like an echo. I resisted the urge to strain to hear what she was saying. I probably didn't want to know anyway. Camden and breathing. That was all I cared about.

No, probably not. But at least you'll know you've tried your best, right? You can go home feeling satisfied.

I guess. I wanted to have some kind of success today. To know I made the right choice. When I opened my eyes, he was staring at me intently. Tracy had moved across the room and was standing right next to me.

"Jesus! You scared the hell out of me. What are you doing?" I yelled.

She leaned on the table in front of me. "I can't believe it."

"What?" I looked back and forth between the two of them. Camden had a huge, goofy grin on his face, but Tracy just looked perplexed.

"I've never heard of someone doing it on the first day," she muttered, almost to herself.

"Me either," Camden said. "We've got a regular prodigy here!" He got up, and it felt like his height and breadth filled the small room completely. Reaching for my hand, he shook it enthusiastically. "Congrats! You did it."

"I did?"

"You did," Tracy answered. "I was talking nonstop that whole time, and you didn't hear a single thing."

"She was slinging some real doozies too," Camden said, pride saturating his voice.

"Like what?"

"That you were a total failure, that you were wasting our time, and that I wanted to go get some dinner before I died," Tracy said, completely deadpan, like the insults meant nothing to her.

And they shouldn't have meant anything to me. She was trying to provoke me. That was her job. But the words still stung. "I'm not a total failure," I said quietly.

"No. You're not," she said. "Far from it." And with that, she patted me on the shoulder and left the room. Camden followed, but not before flashing me another huge smile.

I sat alone in the room in disbelief. I'd done it. I'd actually controlled it.

Someone knocked on the door. "Yeah," I said without looking to see who it was.

"I hear you're a superstar," Owen said, quiet caution mixed with the excitement in his voice.

"I guess." I was still staring at the spot where Camden had been sitting, not quite able to believe it. After all that effort, it had seemed easy, almost natural.

He sat down in Camden's spot, right in my line of sight, so I finally looked at him. "What if I can't do it again tomorrow? I only did it the one time."

Owen laughed. "That's what you're in here worrying about? That you won't be able to do it again?" He dissolved into more laughter.

I crossed my arms over my chest and glared at him. "Why is that funny?"

He straightened up immediately, clearing his throat. "It's not." A smile cracked his face. "Except it is, Mac. No one's ever achieved what you've done this quickly. You're a natural! Of course you'll be able to do it again tomorrow."

"I just wish she hadn't interrupted me, so I could be sure. She scared the hell out of me."

A mischievous smile played on his face. "What did she do to you?"

"She just invaded my personal space."

He leaned in close enough for me to feel his breath on my face. "I'd like to invade your personal space."

I smiled up at him. "Oh, would you now?"

"Maybe."

"We'll see."

"Yes, we will." Our knees touched as he moved his whole body closer. I was tempted to turn my face, just to squash his cocky attitude, but his lips were too tempting. They curled at the corners, since he knew I'd chosen him over my own pride.

The kiss was slow and sweet. I leaned into him, resting my hand on his knee for support.

After a few heartbeats, he pulled back and took a deep breath, as if calming himself. "Well, I'd say it was a pretty good first day on the job after all, wouldn't you?"

"Yes, I would."

"Can I interest you in some dinner? Maybe a movie?"

"Like a date?"

"My, my, you're awfully forward," he said cheekily. "No, I was thinking we could just hang out here with everyone. It'll give you a chance to get to know us all a little. We know you pretty well, so it would be good to even the playing field a little."

"Or maybe I should crawl into a hole and die. Everyone knows all the intimate details about my life."

"Oh, come on. You've got more backbone than that. I know, because I'm not attracted to spineless twits, and I find you very appealing."

I straightened. "Well, I'm certainly not a spineless twit."

"No. I didn't think you were."

"As long as we're clear on that."

His face turned serious as he nodded. "Crystal."

"Good." I stood. "I suppose dinner and a movie wouldn't kill me."

"Glad to see you've let go of the cult-killer theory. We'll just have to make sure it's not a horror movie."

I pushed him as we walked out, causing him to bump into the doorframe and stumble before regaining his balance.

"Got it together there, O?" Mitchell asked from right by the doorway. I hadn't heard his approach, so I was surprised to see him.

"Always."

He nodded and smiled before walking away. I couldn't help but laugh.

"What?" Owen asked.

"You've always got it together? Always?"

If we'd been in one of those cheesy teenage summer flicks, he would've tripped right at that moment. Unfortunately, it was life, not a movie, so he kept his stride. "Don't you forget it."

"Must be nice."

At dinner, everyone flooded me with questions, even though I was pretty sure they already knew most of the answers. Where I was from, what I studied in school, what instruments I played—that sort of thing. They all seemed excited to have a musician join the group, and they begged me to bring my guitar or keyboard or anything to play for them. I told them I wasn't much of a peacock, but if they wanted to sing and have fun, I'd be happy to provide some background music.

"Ok, now it's my turn to ask a question." All eyes were on me. "If you could live forever, what would you do with your life?" It was a fun icebreaker question I'd learned in one of my therapy classes. Every once and a while, someone would really answer it, giving you a glimpse of who they were.

One person said travel. Another said write a book. Someone else claimed they would play all the Mario games back to back.

Once the laughter died down, Owen chimed in, "I wouldn't want to live that long."

"What do you mean?" I asked.

"I don't want to give people the chance to hate me. To become a burden to them. To be—" he hesitated, "—relieved when I die."

"Well, that's one way to kill the mood, O," a guy sitting across from us said.

"Oh, I'm sorry. I meant to say I'd learn to play Gasbag de la Noot."

"Now you're just stealing ideas," I said.

The conversation regained its jovial flow, but I couldn't help wondering what had happened to Owen. Though he always had a smile and a laugh for everyone, he'd given me a glimpse of the dark thoughts that ran deep inside   him.

All night, I kept waiting for the other shoe to drop. I was an outsider. Someone had to hate me, right? Some scorned girl who had her eyes on Owen, some unimpressed person who might perceive me as a threat for my successes today. But they were all welcoming and kind. It made me a little uneasy, particularly since there was still so much I didn't know.

During the movie, Owen took my hand and leaned over. "Would you relax?" he whispered. "We can all hear you wondering which one of us hates you and is covering it up."

I could feel myself turning six shades of red, so I was grateful for the dim lights.

One of the guys I didn't know paused the movie. "Listen, if being readers has taught us anything, it's to be honest and open with the people in our lives. Because everyone else is going to know exactly what you're thinking until you learn to block your thoughts. We've all been where you are." Everyone laughed, and I tried to chuckle with them, swallowing my horror at the intimate facts they knew about me.

The girl sitting on the floor in front of me turned and touched my leg. "Hey. It should make you feel better that we know all that stuff about you and still want hang out with you anyway." She winked at me, and Owen burst out laughing.

I sighed. Clearly, they weren't bothered. I was the one who was going to have to get over this. Maybe I could level the playing field someday, but today, I'd have to settle for my small victory in the training room.

I snuggled into Owen's arm to watch the movie, trying to focus on what tomorrow might bring.

14

My fears were unfounded. The next day, I honed in on Camden like it was nothing, so Tracy added a third person, then a fourth to the group. My next task was to change my focus to a different person's thoughts. Once I figured out how to do it, I could easily zero in on the single voice of my choosing. It didn't seem to matter who it was or how many people were in the room.

By the end of the day, we'd moved out into the gym to accommodate more people. She added Mitchell as a fifth person, and I zoned in on him immediately.

Mitchell, what happened the day we met?

He avoided eye contact with me, scratching the back of his neck, visibly uncomfortable. *What do you mean? You were being attacked, and I thought I'd lend a hand. In retrospect, I'm not sure you needed it.*

Afterwards, though, you acted like you didn't want to have anything to do with me. Like the very sight of me made your skin crawl.

In the back of my mind, I knew the others were listening and trying to distract me, but I didn't care. This was my chance for answers, and I wasn't going to let it pass me by again.

He sighed heavily. *Put yourself in my place, Mac. I knew you were a reader. I also knew you thought you were all alone. I wanted to tell you, I did. But it wasn't the right time, and I wasn't the right person. I needed to get myself away from you before I messed things up.*

I thought about that for a minute. *Things? What things?*

Just things, I don't know. He shrugged in his chair, clearly getting flustered. *There's a protocol to follow with new people, and I didn't want to be responsible for doing it wrong.*

He didn't elaborate and I saw him give Tracy a desperate stare, silently pleading with her to move on. I wondered if the "thing" he meant was David sending Owen to check up on me.

"All right, that's enough. I think that's good for today. Thank you for coming, everyone. We'll see you tomorrow," Tracy said.

The rest of the week went even better. Maddie's supportive do-great-on-your-first-week text messages combined with my successes kept my spirits high. By Friday, all the available members of the Unseen were helping me train in the gym. I could hone in on one person's voice and change my focus at will. I even learned to recognize voices, and zero in on someone with a purpose, instead of just picking someone randomly.

After we finished up on Friday, Tracy dismissed everyone and asked me to meet her in the training room for a debriefing, as she called it.

She sat down across the table from me, then leaned forward and interlaced her hands. "Listen, Mackenzie, I'm going to be honest."

My heartbeat quickened as dread crept into my stomach, feeling heavy, like a rock.

She ignored my panic. "We've covered about a month's worth of material in a week."

"Okay…" *Was that good or bad?*

"I suppose it's good *and* bad. It's more than good; it's

amazing. I've never seen anyone who's as much of a natural as you are. There's still a lot for you to learn, but I'm afraid there will come a time when I can't teach you anything more." Her voice got a little quieter, almost reflective. "I'm not sure what we'll do then."

"Well, it's only been a week. I'm sure we don't need to worry about that already."

"Maybe, maybe not. At any rate, you probably don't need to worry about it at all. You're going to be a great asset to the Unseen."

I'd never thought of that. I could actually be an asset, rather than a bumbling fool everyone and their brother could read.

A rather deadly asset, at that.

"What?" The comment snapped me out of my own mind like someone had cracked a whip next to my head.

"What?" she asked, her face calm.

"You said, 'A rather deadly asset, at that.' What the hell does that mean?"

"Shit. You heard that? I apologize for my carelessness." She left it at that, as if there was nothing more to say on the matter.

I'd never heard her swear before, and it startled me. "But what did you mean?"

"Nothing. Nothing at all. That's enough for today. Truly remarkable work this week, Mackenzie. I look forward to seeing just how far you can push your abilities." She had never been one for social courtesies, but this exit was abrupt, even for her.

I followed her out. "Tracy, wait."

She waved her hand over her back, but she didn't stop walking.

Owen met me halfway across the gym. He raised his voice a little over the clang of the weights being used. "What happened?"

"Tracy said I would be a deadly asset. What the hell does that mean?"

"Oh God, she *said* that to you? I can't believe she would say something like that! Especially without talking to David first."

"No, she thought it. Honestly, I think she forgot to put her wall back up or something. I can't ever read her unless she lets me. She apologized for her carelessness and hustled out of the room."

"Shit."

"That's exactly what she said. What did she mean, Owen? I have a right to know."

He ran a hand down my arm. "I'm sorry, Mac. I don't have the right to tell you."

I turned and walked away from Owen, marching straight to David's door. Knocking loudly, I barged in. "David, listen, it's time to come clean—" I stopped short, finding his office empty.

Owen jogged up behind me. "David is out for the weekend."

"Of course he is."

"Listen, I'm sure Tracy just misspoke. She's very military in her mindset; you'll get used to it. Don't jump to any conclusions, and certainly don't worry about it." His voice was even and reassuring, but his eyes told a different story. They were big, and lines of concern had formed in the outer corners. I wanted to believe him. I needed to believe him. But the alarm bells that Tracy's comment had set off in my head were so loud... and frankly, I wasn't sure silencing them was the right thing to do.

That night we sat on the couch and watched another movie with a few other members of the Unseen. Mitchell was there too, along with two others I hadn't gotten to know yet.

I tried to focus on the movie and watch as Tom Cruise tried to save the world again, but I couldn't.

Owen's right. Tracy was probably just being flippant. Another explosion lit the room up. *When have you ever known Tracy to be flippant?* Music blasted through the surround sound speakers as Tommy narrowly missed dying yet again. *You don't even know Tracy. You've spent five days with her. Just because she slipped up once and let you read her private thoughts means nothing. Everyone thinks dumb things when they think no one can hear them. Even you.*

"Especially you," Owen whispered, and I threw a piece of popcorn at him.

It didn't mean anything. Stop focusing on a five-second comment and concentrate on your successes this week. You should be celebrating, not freaking out. But Owen had reacted strangely when I'd told him about Tracy's comment. *What did he mean when he said he didn't have the right to tell me what she meant?*

A girl in front interrupted my train of thought. "Quiet, Mac. I'm trying to watch this gorgeous hunk of man save humanity."

I snuggled in further to Owen's body and tried to watch the movie, but I couldn't concentrate. My fingers twitched.

"I'm gonna go home," I whispered.

Owen looked startled. "What? Why?"

"I need music. I can't relax."

He smiled. "Why don't you come with me?"

Taking my hand, he led me to the library. No one was in there but us and, off to the side, where there used to be a couch, I spied an upright Steinway. It was a beautiful piece. I went to it instinctually and ran my hand along the top, feeling like I was one with the smooth surface. Owen stood back and watched.

When I sat at the bench, I noticed *Gaspard de la Nuit* ready to go on the music stand. I smiled as I stroked the bright white keys. This was the first time I'd ever sat at a brand-new piano.

What was the meaning of this? Were they trying to buy me? Show me what I could have if I cooperated?

Owen ignored my thoughts, effectively keeping me in

the dark on why the Unseen had essentially bought me an expensive piano. Instead, he asked, "Well, are you going to play?"

"But, this is the library. Won't people be disturbed?"

"We voted, and the group decided the reading experience could only be enhanced by some music. The one or two dissenters said they wouldn't mind going to their rooms if they were truly bothered."

My fingers itched to play as my feet found their way to the pedals. Owen took a seat at the bench next to me. He looked at the music, then back at me, urging me to play.

I wanted to so bad, but I wasn't sure I could accept something like this. What would it mean if I did? What would it mean if I didn't? The questions piled on top of questions were enough, and *Gaspard* flowed from my hands, my fingers dancing along the keys. Music once again filled my mind, as well as the small room where we were sitting.

I wasn't sure how long I played with Owen sitting there next to me, but the exhaustion I felt when I finally stopped indicated it had been a while.

"Sorry. I didn't mean to play for that long. I hope I didn't disturb anyone." I wasn't used to playing somewhere that public. Normally, I played in practice rooms or my own apartment, but there were plenty of people around the Unseen's facility. Embarrassment threatened.

The look on Owen's face was one of total enchantment. I wasn't sure if it was directed at me, or the music.

He smiled and put his hand on my knee. "I think everyone really enjoyed it. I know I did."

I relaxed a little. Hopefully, they would still feel that way in a few weeks, after listening to me play incessantly.

Owen chuckled. "If nothing else, it silenced your constant musings for a bit. I think people were relieved."

I shoved him off the bench. "I should go home."

Owen got up to walk me to my car. He stopped me before I could get in. "Hey, I was wondering if you might want to get together this weekend."

"Oh, yeah?"

"Well, I left you alone last weekend and that was a colossal mistake on my part. This time, I thought I might take a different approach."

"Smart."

He shifted his weight. "So, interested?"

"Like a date?"

"Yeah, like a date."

I hesitated. Actual dating had always gone poorly for me. I'd never gotten past the first date with anyone, and I'd had my fair share of them. The last thing I wanted to do was wreck this growing connection I had with Owen.

"I don't think one date will wreck anything."

"You've never been on a date with me."

"And I intend to remedy that this weekend. How about I take you to the Genghis Grill?"

The shit-ass grin he wore, combined with his comment, made me groan. "Anywhere but there."

"So you'll go out with me?"

I gasped, realizing too late that I'd played right into his verbal trap. "You are an evil genius."

"An evil genius who's going to take you on the best date of your life. I'll see you tomorrow around noon."

"Noon? What kind of date starts at noon?"

"The kind where we get to spend the day together." He shut my car door once I was buckled in, leaning through the window to gently kiss me on the cheek. "I'll see you tomorrow."

"Okay, great," I said. Once I was out of earshot, I added, "I hope."

15

It was after ten when I got home, but I called Maddie anyway. She answered on the first ring.

"Hey stranger! How was your first week?"

We'd been texting all week, but I had been exhausted by the time I got back to my apartment each night, so I hadn't taken the time to call her.

"Pretty good actually. Apparently, I'm some kind of prodigy. I blew through a month's worth of training in a week."

"Whoa, really? That's awesome!"

"Yeah, my trainer said today she's worried she might not have much to teach me soon."

"Good?" She said it like a question.

"Yeah, I don't know what to think either. But she did say I could be an amazing asset to the company if I keep progressing like this." I left out the deadly part. I didn't know what to make of it. There was no need to give fuel to Maddie's very active imagination.

"Man, Mac, that's amazing. Are you feeling pretty good about your decision?"

Tracy's comment kept cycling through my head. "You know, I still feel like there's something huge they're not telling me. It's making it hard for me to settle in completely."

"Oh, really? What makes you say that?"

I scrambled for a half-truth. "I don't know for sure. It's just a feeling I have."

"Your Spidey sense going crazy again?"

"I guess so."

"Well, it's never been wrong before, at least as far as I can remember. But maybe it's nothing. A dumb company policy, like KFC's secret recipe or something. Just because it's a secret doesn't automatically make it bad."

"No, you're right. I should stop assuming the worst. It was a great week, so I should expect great things moving forward."

"Absolutely." She paused. "How's the hot guy?"

"I'm surprised you waited this long to ask me about him."

"Oh my God, it was complete torture."

I laughed. "Owen is great. He's taking me on a date tomorrow."

"A date!" She squealed. "How exciting!"

"But what if this ruins everything? You know how much success I've had with dating."

"Then he wasn't the right guy for you, and you haven't wasted any time on him." She said it so matter-of-factly, like I wouldn't be losing anything if he wasn't the right guy for me. Certainly not my entire world or the air in my lungs, yet the mere thought of it made it difficult to breathe. "Honestly though," Maddie said, "I'd be surprised if that happened."

Oh, good, I thought. *She's throwing me a bone.*

"You haven't said much about him, but I can tell you're enamored with him. That's never happened before! Besides, not everyone's dates crash and burn on day one, you know."

"I suppose you're right," I said. "I just don't want to wreck it."

"So don't."

"You're always so helpful, Maddie."

"Hey, I do what I can. Listen, the bottom line is to have fun, maybe learn a thing or two about him. Just enjoy yourself!" She paused for a moment, and I knew what was coming next.

"What are you going to wear?" She plowed into the normal rundown, not missing a beat. But for the first time ever, I actually cared. What *was* I going to wear? I wasn't sure what I should be more worried about, the fact that I actually wanted to look good for Owen, or the fact that Maddie knew it.

After another thirty minutes of frantic discussion, we settled on a flowy skirt paired with a white blouse and white sandals, with a white headband, beaded earrings, and a pearl necklace for accessories. I would do my makeup meticulously, and then send her a picture for approval.

Our planning session complete, the only thing left for me to do was go on the actual date.

Owen knocked on my door promptly at noon. I wondered if he'd been standing out there for a few minutes just so he could be right on time.

When I opened the door he said, "I wasn't."

"Well, you're very punctual then."

He looked me up and down. "You should change."

I had spent much longer than I usually did on my appearance, so his comment was devastating. "Why?" was all I could choke out.

"Because we're going swimming and hiking. I wouldn't want you to ruin that pretty skirt."

Nice save, I thought.

"Thank you." He tipped his head to me, and I rolled my eyes.

"Well, if you'd provided me with an itinerary, I would've dressed appropriately."

He shrugged. "I like an element of surprise. It's

romantic."

"Romantic, stressful, whichever."

He laughed. "Hurry up and change, or we'll miss the next tour."

I invited him in to sit on the couch while I changed. "Tour? What tour?" I called out from behind the closed bedroom door while I frantically searched for a swimsuit that wasn't totally threadbare and appropriate hiking clothes. *A swimsuit? Seriously? On our first date? This is a nightmare. I don't want to be half naked in front of him already!* My heart skipped a beat. *Okay, maybe I do a little bit.*

"Just FYI, the door provides little-to-no soundproofing for your thoughts."

I sank to the floor and covered my head with a shirt I was about to cast aside. "Good to know," I called from underneath it. *You knew that. If he were a normal person, you'd be able to hear him almost through the whole damn apartment because it's so small. Use your head.*

After a few minutes of wallowing in humiliation, I tucked in my bottom lip, gathered my things, and opened the door. I was dressed in a T-shirt, shorts, and trainers, with my nicest bikini underneath.

"Better?"

"For what we're doing today? Yes."

"A very diplomatic answer."

"I'll take that as a compliment," he said as he stood and walked with me to the door.

"Just how public is this place you're taking me?" I asked him, feeling naked outside without my iLs.

"Consider it a hidden gem of Florida. There will be people there, but I don't expect it to be crowded. You should be able to manage. If you have trouble, I'm sure I can come up with something for you to focus on," he said confidently.

My snappy comeback caught in my throat when he stopped in front of a brand-new BMW. The only thing I knew about them was that they were expensive. Really expensive. I couldn't even tell what model it was.

"Jeez, this is a nice car," I said.

"Yeah, the Unseen has two of them. Lucky for me, one was available today." He opened my door and I slipped inside, settling into the plush leather seat. Suddenly, I was glad I hadn't taken too long getting changed. The leather was still cool from his drive over. "So, where are we going?"

"That's need-to-know information, and right now, you don't need to know," he said as he buckled his seat belt and started the car. After punching a classical music station on the radio, he hit the road.

I raised my eyebrows. "Trying to make points?"

"No, I like this."

"Oh, really? What is it?"

"Gasbag de la noot," he said confidently.

If I'd had a drink, I would've spit it all over the dashboard laughing.

I stared out the window, watching as the landscape changed from city to country. I'd never been out this way before. Suddenly, the need to ask him something that had been on my mind for a while became insurmountable. "Owen, can I ask you something?"

"You just did. Clearly, you're capable."

I glared at him, but he just looked straight ahead, feigning innocence.

"Why do you like me?" I finally asked.

"What kind of question is that?"

"I don't know. I'm used to being able to read the men I date. I know what their intentions are right from the beginning." I looked out the window and lowered my voice. "Anyway, I know why I'm attracted to you. And I'm pretty sure you know it too. But I have no idea why you're interested in me."

He was silent for what seemed like miles. *Good. I ruined everything before we even got to the date.*

He snorted. "You didn't ruin anything. I was just

trying to think of something intelligent to say because *I* don't want ruin it."

"Oh, Lord. Then I'll be waiting all day."

"That."

"What?"

"That's why I like you."

I opened my mouth to respond, but the words caught in my throat. *My snark? He likes me for my snark?*

"Exactly." He smiled as he watched the road, seemingly content.

Itching to know more about him, I thought I'd bait him. "You know, Maddie's pretty snarky too. You'd like her. She's like a sister to me. My only family, really. Are you close with your family?"

It was subtle, but his expression tightened. "No."

Wondering if this was the reason for the darkness inside him, I probed a little more. "How come?"

He stared straight ahead, his knuckles white from his tight grip on the steering wheel. "Because they're dead."

"What do you know? Mine are too. That's something we have in common," I said, trying to lighten the mood. He didn't respond. I lowered my voice. "What happened?"

"Today is not the day for that story." He didn't take his eyes off the road as he said it.

We were quiet for the rest of the ride. After just under an hour of driving, we pulled into a state park.

By the time we arrived, Owen had visibly relaxed and I hoped his mood was improving.

Florida Caverns, the sign read.

All the years I'd lived in Tallahassee, I'd never heard of the place. "So it's a state park?"

"Yup! Only the coolest state park around. My parents brought my little brother and me here one summer. We had a great time," he said, genuine excitement in his voice. He parked the car and got out. "Come on. Just wait till you see!"

He led me to the main building. So far, it looked similar to most Florida state parks, complete with dense woods and ample parking. I was sure there was a watering hole somewhere too—there always was.

A bell jingled overhead when we walked in the door. "Welcome to Florida Caverns," the man behind the counter said. "What can I do for you?"

"What time is the next tour?"

"Starting in five minutes. You've got good timing."

"Perfect!" Owen looked over at me, mischief in his eyes. "Good thing you didn't take any more time to wallow in your bedroom."

I hated him for bringing up that little gem of a moment. "Yes, well, give it time. You're sure to do something worthy of wallowing before the day is out."

He chuckled. "You're very confident about that."

"I know my audience."

"Do you?" Something about the way he said it made me pause.

"No, I suppose I don't," I said quietly. "But that sure as hell isn't my fault." The anger in my voice surprised me.

"You're right," he said, and turned to the smiling man behind the counter, who was obviously entertained by our exchange. "What time is the next tour?"

"It'll be at two."

"We'll be back then."

I glanced at my watch—two o'clock was an hour away. "But we're here now. Don't you want to go on this one?"

He took my hand and led me out of the building. "I want to do this more."

He found a secluded patch of grass in the shade, facing the crystal-clear water. It was beautiful. A staircase led down into the watering hole, where people of all ages swam and splashed. It called to me. Despite the shade, the Florida heat was gathering sweat between my breasts and dripping into my bra. I resisted the urge to dab at it with my shirt. That would only leave a big, ugly wet mark.

We sat in silence, watching the swimmers for what felt like an eternity. Finally, I couldn't stand it any longer. "Care to go for a swim? I'm dying here."

"I know you deserve more than what I've given you."

His words caught me off guard, despite his snap decision to wait for the later tour. "That's probably true," I said, "but you'll have to be more specific."

He smiled with one corner of his mouth as he watched the swimmers. "I know it upsets you that you know basically nothing about me." He turned and looked into my eyes. There was pain in his dark gaze, but he blinked and it was gone, replaced by resolve.

Now that he'd raised the subject, I didn't want to let him off the hook. "It does bother me. Frankly, if you want to have any kind of relationship with me, it should bother you too."

He nodded and looked back out at the swimmers. I followed his gaze. Everyone was having such a nice day. We should be enjoying ourselves too.

"Time. I just need time," he said, his voice little more than a whisper.

"Time? We don't have any time!" I shouted.

He turned to look at me, eyes wide with surprise... and pain.

I stood and grabbed his hands, pulling him to his feet. "This day is melting away, and we're wasting it up here in the shade!" Relief washed over his face as I pulled him close to me, just barely holding on to both of his hands. I lowered my voice. "Take all the time you need." I kissed him lightly on the lips. "You just better hope I'm still around when you're ready." I smiled devilishly at him and ran down to the water line.

"If that's the fastest you can run, I'll be able to catch up to you anyway!" he called after me.

We splashed and swam in the cold spring water for nearly an hour, almost missing the next tour. I was famished when we got out, so Owen bought us some snacks at the little store. We munched quickly, as no food or drinks were allowed in the caverns.

My heartbeat quickened as I jammed the last chip into my mouth, tossed the bag into the trash can, and jogged to catch up to the back of the group heading for the caverns. I'd never known Florida had caverns. Our home state was so sandy; I sort of assumed anything underground would just collapse on itself.

The entrance to the cavern was little more than a slit between two rocks. We squeezed through and were greeted by the most amazing formations I'd ever seen— the result of thousands of years of work by Mother Nature. I gasped as I took it all in—stalagmites and stalactites formed columns all around us. The park had even used special lighting in some areas to make the formations colorful. Bats clung to the ceiling, and we ducked low in some areas to avoid disturbing them.

The temperature dropped markedly as we ventured further into the cave. The tour guide had embarked on a long monologue explaining the formations and the history of the caverns, but I wasn't listening. I was too busy soaking it all in. In some spots, if you looked closely, you could almost see the faces of trolls in the ancient formations. I wondered if there were any folktales about them.

Maybe you'd know the answer if you were listening to the tour guide, Owen chided from behind his smile.

And you were listening to him because you're the good one, right?

No, your thoughts were too noisy. I couldn't hear the guy.

I cocked an eyebrow at him. *Sounds like you need to spend a little more time with Tracy to learn how to tune unwanted voices out.*

Who said you were unwanted? He winked at me, and my knees went weak.

Wanting to prove myself to Owen, I focused on the

guide. I entered his mind easily, with much less effort than it took with other readers. With them, it was like an unlocked door stood in my way. All I had to do was open it. But with the guide, there wasn't even a superficial barrier. I just waltzed right in.

I scanned his mind, searching for the information I wanted. It took me a moment, since there was a plethora of information in there about his family, his job, and the games he was currently playing. Eventually, I reached his knowledge about the caverns, which was fairly extensive.

Hmm. Nothing about trolls. But he does know a disturbing story about some kind of picnic shooting where a kid died in the eighteen hundreds.

He didn't answer me. When I looked over at him, he was staring at me.

"What?"

"You amaze me."

I beamed. "Don't you forget it."

We spent the rest of the tour holding hands when we could. When we finally left the caverns behind, the sun seemed oppressively bright. I squinted and held my head up in a feeble attempt to shield myself from it.

"Well, what now?" I said through my scrunched-up face.

"Head home for dinner?"

"Sounds good. I'm starving." Then I looked down at myself. My clothes were stiff in places from dried sweat and my hair was a tangled mess from swimming. I imagined I didn't smell all that great either, despite our dip in the cool spring. "Um. Where are we going?"

"Don't worry, I thought we'd order a pizza and watch a movie."

I sagged with relief. "Sounds perfect." When we got back into the car, a wave of exhaustion washed over me from all the sun and fresh air. I was asleep before we hit the highway.

I dreamed of Owen. He was holding me in his arms, and there was nothing but him and me… until Tracy's voice seeped in. At first, it was quiet, nothing more than a whisper. *A rather deadly asset.* She said it over and over again, until Owen melted away and her words were the only thing that surrounded me. *A rather deadly asset. A rather deadly asset. A rather—*

Owen woke me up with a start. "Sorry. We're home." He looked concerned.

"Oh, thanks," I said, trying to shake the dream.

"Want to tell me what that was about?" he asked as we walked into my apartment.

"You didn't see?"

"No. Dreams are different."

"Different how?" I asked, tossing my keys into the bowl on the coffee table.

"I don't remember many of the specifics. It's been a while since I studied dreams, but the basic gist is the brain functions differently while you're sleeping. When you dream, you sort of automatically protect yourself against readers."

"Huh. Weird." Consciously blocking others was supposedly a very difficult skill to acquire. It was also the next thing I would be learning.

I went into my bedroom, changing out of my swimsuit and sweaty clothes while Owen ordered the pizza. Resisting the urge to put on sweatpants and a giant T-shirt, I opted for shorts and a tight cotton V-neck shirt—casual, but sexy.

"Pizza will be here in thirty minutes," he said when I came out.

"Sounds great." I settled in next to him on the couch and used the remote to pull up Netflix. "What do you want to watch?"

"You," he said, staring into my eyes. Despite the fact that I couldn't read him, it didn't take a rocket scientist to know what he had in mind.

My body leaned in toward him, but my mind screamed against it. We both stiffened. "Sorry," I said, knowing he must have heard my thoughts. "We can't move this quickly if you're not ready to tell me your secrets." I looked at him, hoping my next words wouldn't hurt him. "I can't trust you right now." *I'm apparently hell-bent on ruining this date,* I thought, not intending for him to hear.

He took my hand. "No. You're not. And I respect you for it."

We started watching the first Harry Potter movie, ate the pizza, and then snuggled close after we finished it. Because it was still early when the movie was over, we started *The Chamber of Secrets,* and went for a double feature. It was only 9:30 when *that* ended, so we decided to go for a triple play. But I drifted off toward the end of *The Prisoner of Azkaban.*

I woke up, and the clock on the cable box blinked 4:02. Owen had his arm draped over me, leaning back against the arm of the couch. He was breathing heavily. I knew he was dead asleep, just like I'd been moments before.

"Owen." My voice was thick with sleep.

"Mmm." He stirred, but he didn't wake up.

"Owen, it's four am. Do you think you should go?"

His eyes came open. "Do you want me to?"

"Well, no, but I didn't know if there were any rules about staying out all night."

He smiled and pulled me closer. "I'm a big boy. They won't miss me after one night."

I snuggled into his chest, breathing in his clean scent. "I'm not so sure about that."

The next time I woke up, the clock showed 7:00—earlier than I normally liked to get up, but I was sore from sleeping in such an awkward position for so long. Still, I didn't want to move. Owen had his arm draped over me, and I rested my head on his chest and listened to his heartbeat. Strong and steady.

I hadn't planned for Owen to spend the night, and all I had for breakfast was cereal. Slowly, I tried to get up without disturbing him, but he stirred and grabbed me, holding me to him tightly.

"Where do you think you're going?" he asked without opening his eyes.

"To see if I can find something other than Froot Loops to eat for breakfast."

"What?" he said, jostling me. "You have Froot Loops? I haven't had those in forever. Is there enough for both of us?"

"Uh, sure." Despite the fact that Froot Loops was one of my favorite cereals, I decided to tease him a little for his enthusiasm. "What, you can't have delicious sugary cereals at home?" I asked.

It felt funny calling it home, but in truth, that was what it was—for Owen, at least. If I couldn't have my cereal there, it sure as heck wouldn't ever be *my* home.

"It's not that we can't. It's that no one else likes them, so they go stale before I can finish a box. I hate to waste it, you know?" He stood behind me while I poured him a bowl. He looked like a little kid at Christmas, hardly able to contain his excitement.

"I judge you a little for not being able to finish a box of cereal on your own."

He threw up his hands in surrender. "Don't judge! I like it, but I'm not exactly a cereal fiend."

We sat on the couch, enjoying our cereal. "What's the plan for today?" I asked.

"No plan. Although, I should get back to help with the Sunday chores."

"Sunday chores?"

"Just dumb stuff. Laundry and cleaning and whatnot."

"Oh, I suppose I should do that too. And apparently go to the grocery store, since all I have to offer my guests is Froot Loops."

He laughed. "Whatever. This is the best breakfast I've had in a while."

I shrugged, pouring myself another bowl. "Whatever twists your Twizzler, man."

When we were finished and we'd cleared the dishes, it seemed like a natural time to part ways, but we were both reluctant. He lingered in the doorway while I picked at the paint on the frame.

"Well, thanks for a great date." I paused for a minute. "My first one."

"What? No, it wasn't. That guy Mitchell chased off, that was a date."

"Not my first date, you goofball. My first *great* date."

He opened his mouth to respond, but nothing came out. Eventually, he shrugged. "Well, you're welcome. I had a pretty awesome time too."

"Oh, good." Apparently, I was out of snappy comebacks for the moment.

"All right, well…" He trailed off.

"Well." I paused, waiting to see if he'd fill in the gap. He didn't. "I guess I'll see you tomorrow then."

"See you tomorrow." He turned to go, but he thought better of it. Sweeping me in his arms, he leaned in for a soft, warm, turn-your-legs-to-Jell-O kiss. When he set me back down, I wasn't sure my body would support its own weight.

I cleared my throat and made a feeble attempt at smoothing my hair. "See you."

An impish grin spread across his face as he walked away.

I spent the rest of the day talking to Maddie on the phone, doing laundry, cleaning the apartment, and alternating between my keyboard and guitar. Maddie fully approved of the details of our date, demanding to know when she would get to meet Owen. The thought filled me with both excitement and dread. Just imagining the two of them in a battle of the wits was enough to give me an anxiety attack. I put her off for the moment, urging her to cool off since I was too busy with training to get away, plus Owen and I had only been on one date. She was disappointed, but she let it go.

That night, I lay in bed thinking of how different my life was from this time two weeks ago. Despite the fact that I wasn't following the path I'd laid out for myself, I felt like I was in the right place. Owen didn't hurt that feeling. But Tracy's voice still nagged at me, reminding me that there was so much I didn't know. Tracy. David. Owen. Mitchell. They were all keeping something from me, and I felt like it was something big. I rolled over and took a deep breath. The only way to uncover the truth was to keep training, show them I was loyal and trustworthy, and let the pieces fall where they may. I just hoped I wouldn't be in the way of any of them when they came crashing down.

16

Monday morning, Tracy didn't waste any time. "As you know, we're going to concentrate on blocking this week. There are two stages to blocking. The first, you know how to do. You've done it before."

"I have." It was an unsure statement, not a question.

"You have. When you focus in on one voice, you block all others out. All you need to do this time is block out that last voice."

I chuckled uneasily. "Sounds like a breeze."

"It's not. Most people take months to get it down. But I know a few people are hoping you'll catch on more quickly."

I think they're tired of listening to your incessant questions, she thought.

Yes, well I'm tired of them too. Maybe if someone around here would give me some answers, they'd get some relief.

She didn't flinch. *Or maybe if you worked a little harder, we wouldn't have to worry about it. Do you plan on getting to work at some point today?*

Oh. We already started? Of course, we started. Like you would have small talk with me.

No, I don't do small talk. She didn't crack a smile, but I

138

would have believed her anyway. *And I certainly don't have small talk when I should be working.*

Despite her harsh exterior, I was really starting to like Tracy. She was rough around the edges, and maybe in between too, but she was honest. Although she hadn't said what she meant when she called me a "deadly asset," she hadn't lied about it either.

We went back and forth all morning with no luck. Owen met me in the gym, as usual.

I couldn't help but notice there weren't as many people in the kitchen as there normally were. "Where's Mitchell? And Camden?"

Owen set his plate down on the table and sat next to me. "They had to go do some work."

"Like off-site?"

"Yeah. On assignment."

"Will I have to do that kind of thing?"

"Probably."

I wondered what exactly that meant. Would I be following people around, recording their thoughts? Stealing secrets? I frowned, hoping it wasn't anything that sinister.

By the time I returned to Tracy, I was almost in a tailspin with my musings.

Tracy insisted I concentrate and get to work. I sighed. *I guess I'll have to puzzle it out later.*

Yes, please.

I tried to block her out for the rest of the afternoon, but without another voice to concentrate on, I floundered.

As usual, a group of us watched a movie together that night, and I noticed just how many of the core group was missing. Seemed like at least five people were gone. I wondered again about where they were, what they were doing. Top-secret mind reading business, no doubt. But what exactly was top-secret mind reading business? Were they getting information for someone? Was the benefactor someone with a lot of enemies who he kept in line using our abilities? Were they doing something illegal? Or perhaps they were working for the government?

I couldn't help feeling discouraged as I tried to fall asleep that night. I hadn't made any progress on blocking, and I didn't know what my future held at this mystery company I was technically "working" for.

A thought struck me so suddenly that I sat up in bed. I couldn't block Tracy because there were no other voices to focus on. No other voices, except my own.

I wonder...

Glancing at the clock, I cursed the late hour. I wanted to test my theory out right away, but it would have to wait.

In the morning, I was more ready to work than ever. I had trouble paying much attention to Owen when he greeted me out front, not wanting to waste any time.

"What's your deal today?" he asked me.

"Nothing. I just want to get started."

"You've got plenty of time, Mac."

"I didn't do very well yesterday, and I want to devote as much time as I can to doing better."

"Seriously, you put too much pressure on yourself. Tracy told you it takes most people at least a month to get blocking. It was no surprise to anyone but you that you couldn't do it on your first day."

I didn't answer. What could I say? Maybe he was right. But as far as I could tell, there was no reason for it to take people that long.

He left me in the gym, as always, and wished me good luck. I nodded, and he laughed.

"Seriously, Mac, lighten up a little bit. It'll be okay, I promise."

I gave him a small smile, but it was fake. From the look on his face, he knew it. "I'll see you for lunch," I said, giving up and going to meet Tracy.

We got right to work. She started in with her usual tactics, telling me how I needed to work harder.

At first, it was hard not to hear her. Hers was the only other voice in the room. But I concentrated on my breathing, and listened to my own thoughts, which had of course gone blank for the moment. I purposefully thought about stupid things—the color of the walls in the training room, how uncomfortable the chair was, just how much time I'd had to spend in that uncomfortable chair lately.

Suddenly, I realized I couldn't hear her. Afraid to ruin it, I didn't search for her voice. I just kept concentrating on my own thoughts. She let me go on like that for quite some time—the whole morning, in fact.

"I think we should get some lunch. When we come back, there will be more people here."

"Oh, okay. How come?"

"Surprisingly, you did it. You successfully blocked me out. Now, you have to practice with a large group."

I smiled to myself.

"Don't get cocky," she said. "It's very difficult to block out a large group. It can be overwhelming."

I thought of the handful of times I'd been caught without my iLs, and a shiver spread through my body. "I'm familiar with the concept."

She nodded. "Eat a good lunch. When we come back, the real work begins."

Great, I thought. *What the hell does that mean?*

"So, you did it?" Owen asked me over lunch.

"I did."

"After one day." He phrased it like a statement, not a question.

"After one day," I repeated.

He was dumbfounded.

"You seem to have forgotten what a valuable asset I am," I said, munching on some chips.

"Apparently," he said, his mouth still hanging open a little.

"Don't you believe me?"

"Of course, I believe you. I mean, it's not like you can lie to me and get away with it for long." He nudged me with his elbow. "It's just so—" he paused, searching for the right word, "—astounding."

"Good?"

"Great, Mac! It's great! I wonder if David knows yet. I bet he'll be antsy to get you to work." I could tell he immediately regretted saying it. He stuffed his mouth full of food to avoid continuing the thought.

Feeling merciful, I decided to let it go. I'd find out what the work was soon, and in the light of day, that was enough for me.

Tracy made good on her promise, and when I came back, there were five people milling around the gym, all people I didn't know that well, since Mitchell and the others were still not on base.

"Okay, let's get started," she announced. Seated in a circle, they bombarded me with their thoughts. Each voice was individual, unique, and blaringly loud. I decided Tracy had told them to do that on purpose to make it hard for me.

I won't lie—it wasn't easy. But I focused on my breathing and my own voice, resisting the urge to find out more about each of these new people by listening to them, and tuned them out. Slowly, the voices became softer, less individualized, and more like white noise. Eventually, they faded away completely and I was left alone in my head, so to speak.

One of the guys laughed out loud.

"Don't break her concentration," Tracy said.

"I'm sorry. It's very impressive," he said. "She hasn't even been here two weeks and she's doing things some of us are still learning how to do."

"Wait, who's still learning?" I asked. "I thought I was low man on the totem pole."

"You are," Tracy said, not willing to let me forget it.

"And you need to focus on yourself without worrying where others are in their training. Worry about where *you* are with *your* training."

Typical Tracy answer. "It's a bit early to break for the day, so we might start on stage two today. Thank you all for your help. You're dismissed."

They got up in unison, no one daring to ignore Tracy. She got up and went into the training room, and I followed automatically.

"It seems you're already ready for stage two," she said, closing the door while I took a seat.

"What's stage two?"

"Stage one is learning to block other people's thoughts, which may or may not be directed at you."

"Right…" I trailed off, not sure where she was going with this.

"Stage two is pushing out someone who's inside your mind. Another reader who you don't want there."

"Inside my mind? Like how?"

"Readers can take many forms. They can be obvious, or they can hide in the shadows of your mind, stealing your thoughts. It's imperative for you to learn to guard yourself against other readers."

"Steal my thoughts? Why? Who would want them? All I think about is Owen and doing well at training."

She frowned in disapproval. "Yes, well, eventually you may expand your horizons. In which case, you could be a very interesting target indeed. Someone might want insight into how you're going through the training process this quickly, so they can duplicate your method and rapidly create some kind of army."

"That sounds like something you would do."

"Indeed." She nodded. "So you can see why it's important to learn to guard your mind."

"I suppose. I guess I'm not as distrustful as you are, though. I don't really think anyone would want to see inside my mind. You know how messy it is in there."

"The day may come when you've had reason to become as distrustful as I am. And if it does, it's best to be ready."

I frowned, a little disturbed. Why did everyone here have such a dismal worldview? I preferred to think the best of most people until they proved me wrong, which usually didn't take very long given my abilities as a reader. Seeing people's innermost thoughts told you right away what kind of person they truly were. To be honest, most people were selfish but good-natured. I supposed you couldn't ask for much more than that. So, despite the fact that I didn't understand how necessary this last step was, I pushed forward anyway.

"What do I do?"

First, you must learn to feel others in your mind, she thought.

I had never pictured myself in someone else's mind. For me, it had always been more like overhearing someone who was talking too loud, not an intentional invasion of privacy. The guide popped into my head. *That* hadn't been overhearing. I had deliberately searched his brain for information.

"You did what?" Tracy demanded.

"What?"

"You searched someone's mind for information?"

"Technically, I suppose I did." Feeling like I was in trouble, I tried to keep it vague, although I wasn't sure to what end. If she wanted to know exactly what had happened, it was all there, plain as day.

"Did you get what you were looking for?"

"No."

Her eyes narrowed. "Is that because he didn't have what you were looking for?"

"I suppose so, yes." Neither one of us said anything for a while. She glanced at her watch and frowned.

"I think we will break early today. I need to speak to David. We will pick back up here tomorrow." She stood abruptly and went to the door.

"Tracy, wait." She stopped. "Did I do something wrong?"

"No, I'm afraid you've done everything right." But there was no smile, no excitement, and no encouragement.

"That's convincing," I said, but she'd turned and left before I could respond, leaving me alone with my words.

Owen wasn't waiting in the gym like usual, and I assumed it was because our meeting had ended early. I ventured upstairs on my own, searching for him, but he wasn't in the kitchen, library, or the living room. Finally, I asked someone. I found one of the guys who had worked with Tracy and me that afternoon. He was sitting in the TV room, watching something.

"Hey, have you seen Owen?"

"Yeah, he's in his room with Mitchell," he said, not looking up at me.

"The others are back?"

"Guess so." Clearly, he wasn't interested. I was.

I took the stairs two at a time, nearly falling onto the landing. Not sure what was driving my sudden urge to see Mitchell, I pounded on Owen's door, hoping they'd be together.

Owen opened it partway. "Hey. You're done early. Listen, this isn't really a good time. If you want, I'll meet you upstairs in a little while. Otherwise, I'll see you tomorrow, okay?"

"The others told me they were back. I want to see him." I knew Mitchell wouldn't tell me anything about where he'd been, if for no other reason than his apparent discomfort around me, but I had to try. The curiosity was eating at me.

He looked over his shoulder, I assumed at Mitchell. He squeezed through the door out into the hallway, opening it wide enough for me to catch a glimpse of Mitchell. He was lying on Owen's bed, ashen faced and unconscious. The sight took my breath away.

"What the hell happened? Is he okay? Should we take him to the hospital?"

"Settle down and lower your voice for God's sake. I just got him to sleep." He said it protectively, like Mitchell was his child or something.

I crossed my arms over my chest as I waited for an answer, but Owen just stood there. Exasperated, I threw my arms in the air. "What can I do to help?"

The look on his face softened. "I need you to stay out of it. Mitchell will be fine. That has to be enough for now."

"He doesn't look fine to me." I stood on my tiptoes, trying to peer over Owen's shoulder, but he'd shut the door most of the way, preventing me from seeing inside.

He took my arm and led me down the hallway, away from his door. "Why are you done early?"

"I don't really want to talk about it." *You insist on keeping secrets? Well, so do I.*

He pinched the bridge of his nose. "That's fine. I need to get back to Mitchell." He reached for my hand, but I kept it just out of reach. He acted like he didn't notice. "I'll see you tomorrow, okay?" His tone was friendly, but final.

I didn't respond. No, it was not okay. Clearly, it was anything but okay. Whatever had happened to Mitchell was pretty awful. I wondered about Camden and the others, but I didn't know them well enough to go poking around.

I stood alone on the landing, debating whether to go home, or to try and get answers from David. The more I thought about it, the more I was leaning toward going home. If David was the man I thought he was, he'd be with the people who'd just returned. They needed him more than I did right now. And to go barging into his office, demanding answers, when his employees were potentially in a state of crisis, was a bit childish.

In the end, I opted to go home. But my apartment was lonelier than ever. What had happened today? Now, more than ever, I felt like I was an outsider of this group I'd given up everything to join. And for what? Questions swirled in my head, my only companions for the rest of the night.

17

The next day, Owen was waiting for me in his usual spot. I decided to give him the cold shoulder. Immature? Perhaps. Did I feel better, walking past him with my head held high, saying nothing? Absolutely.

He trailed behind me as I brushed by. "Well, good morning to you!" he called from behind me.

I ignored him and descended the stairs, heading straight for Tracy.

"Hey, Mackenzie, wait up!" He huffed behind me, but I stayed ahead.

When we reached the second landing, he grabbed my arm. "Hey." He turned me to face him.

I hoped icicles would sprout on his nose from the frosty glare I gave him.

"What's wrong?"

The genuine concern on his face gave me pause. Maybe he didn't deserve this. Then I remembered the way he'd brushed me off, and my resolve turned to steel. "What's wrong? You can give me the cold shoulder, but you can't take it?"

"Mac, I wasn't giving you the cold shoulder yesterday."

The memory of Mitchell lying in that bed, his skin a bizarre ashen shade, came rushing back to me. "Is Mitchell okay?"

"I told you last night that he was."

I frowned at his slightly curt answer. At least, I thought it was curt. "So you did."

We stood on the landing in a stalemate. Him with his secrets, me with my anger.

"Listen, I'm sorry if you got your feelings hurt last night. The only reason I can't talk to you about what happened is because you're still a new recruit. You can't know everything yet. But I promise... there will come a day when you do know everything. No secrets." He came closer to me and took both my hands in his. "And when that day comes, I can only hope you'll stick around to share them with me."

Tracy came up the stairs at just that moment. "There you are. We need to get to work. There's a lot to do today."

I nodded, not breaking eye contact with Owen, unsure if I was nodding at him or Tracy. Maybe both of them. While Tracy and I descended the last set of stairs, my mind circled around what Owen had said. What secrets did he have that would make me want to leave? I couldn't shake the feeling that it had something to do with the work of the Unseen. What exactly had he done for them?

Tracy shut the door behind me a little hard, startling me out of my Owen-centered world. "I need you to focus today. What I'm asking you to do isn't easy. And you'll never be successful at it if you aren't one-hundred-percent focused."

I nodded. "Fair enough." Taking a deep breath, I worked hard to push Owen from my mind.

"Now, as I said yesterday, you'll need to work to feel me in your mind. Then, shut me out. Protect yourself."

The way she emphasized 'protect yourself' made one question spring to my mind. *From what?*

Everyone, she thought.

We nodded to each other, and I knew it was time to get to work. I cleared my mind, trying to 'find her,' but nothing seemed different. It was still my mind. I couldn't hear her thoughts, but I wasn't sure if that was because she wasn't thinking, or because I was blocking her. Everything was still so new.

With nothing to listen to but my own thoughts, my mind tried to wander back to Owen, and I had to re-center several times. I searched and searched for any sign of her. Something out of place, unfamiliar. Then, finally, I thought I felt something odd. Like a shadow from a streetlight that wasn't there.

I had my eyes shut, but I heard Tracy shift in her seat. "Good," she said aloud. I opened my eyes and saw her leaning toward me. "Now, work to push me out. Overpower me. Take back control of your thoughts."

I tried to do what she said, but it was too abstract. Once I'd found her, she stuck out like a sore thumb, but I had no idea how to 'overpower' her. I took a deep breath before I began. Then, starting in the far corner of my mind, as far away from her as I could get, I spread out my thoughts slowly, like pouring caramel from a jar. They poured through my mind, claiming every nook and cranny. At last, I came to her and washed over her like a giant wave in an angry sea.

When I was finished, I couldn't detect any trace of her. Either she'd moved somewhere else, or I'd succeeded in flushing her out. I opened my eyes, looking to her for the answer.

She stared at me, blank-faced.

"Should we try again?" My stomach grumbled in response.

Tracy looked at her watch. "No need. I apologize. I wasn't watching the time, and it's three o'clock already. Why don't we just call it a day?" She started to get up, but I stopped her.

"Tracy, wait. Did I do it? Was that right?"

"Mackenzie, that was one-hundred-percent correct. I will see you tomorrow."

Owen was working out in the gym when I came out. "You missed lunch."

"I just now realized that."

"What happened?"

"I pushed Tracy out."

"Like you physically pushed her out the door? Looked to me like she walked out on her own."

I smiled at him in spite of myself, sick of being angry with him for his secrets. "No. I pushed her out of my mind."

"What?" He stopped in his tracks in the middle of the staircase, turning to look at me. "What do you mean? Explain it to me like I'm an idiot."

"Shouldn't be that hard."

He ignored my joke, and I shifted my weight uncomfortably. What was the big deal?

"The big deal is that it took most of us the better part of a year to learn how to do that. You're saying Tracy entered your mind, you found her, and then pushed her out. In a day?"

"More or less, yes."

His mouth hung open. "I'm not sure I believe you." He said it quietly, as if it were some kind of swear word.

I bristled. "Fine. Let's go. Right now."

"What? What do you mean?"

I sat down cross-legged on the stairs and pulled on his arm, forcing him to sit down in front of me. We were facing each other, our backs against the wall in the middle of the staircase.

He stared at me intently, and I stared right back, waiting. "Are we really going to do this?"

"Are you scared or something?" I challenged.

Frowning, he turned silent. I knew he'd started.

He wasn't nearly as elegant as Tracy. His formless shadow was huge, and I found him right away. I smiled to myself when I heard him straighten. He knew I'd found him. Slowly, just as I'd done with Tracy, I overwhelmed him with my thoughts. In the end, we only ended up sitting there for ten minutes or so.

"Holy shit," Owen whispered. "Do you know what this means?"

"Apparently you do."

"You could be the most gifted reader in history."

"There were mind readers in history?"

"That's the question you're asking me right now?"

I shrugged my shoulders. "I guess so."

"Of course there were. Readers didn't just appear out of nowhere."

"Like who?"

"Anne Boleyn is one of the most famous readers. She didn't play her cards quite right, so she was beheaded after being accused of bewitching the king—which was absolutely true, except she was using mind reading, not sorcery."

I leaned back against the wall, questioning the extent of my historical knowledge, wondering how many readers were hiding among the 'normal' people.

"Wait, how did she bewitch the king, if she was just a reader?"

"There's more to reading than just hearing people's thoughts. I expect you'll be learning that from Tracy soon." He stood up and offered me his hand.

"So tell me who else we owe our legacy to," I said, excited to know we were connected with famous figures of history.

His expression turned dark. "Jim Jones is the most recent reader to come to fame."

I didn't know the name off the top of my head.

"The leader of the Jonestown cult."

I recoiled as I remembered the people who'd killed

themselves and their own children after being brainwashed.

"Yeah. It wasn't our finest moment. Jones was a talented reader, obviously. He killed those we sent to see exactly what he was up to."

I searched my limited knowledge on the event. "Wasn't there a senator he killed?"

"That's the one."

The thought that there were readers in government office was overwhelming and intriguing at the same time.

We walked the rest of the way in silence while I chewed on the new historical facts. But, before we headed into the common room, he turned and looked at me. "Do you understand the impact you could have on the world of readers?"

I frowned and shook my head.

He took my face in both of his hands. "You will."

The next day, Tracy was as serious as ever, despite the progress I'd made. You'd think I would get a day off, perhaps some accolades. Nope.

"Let's get to work," she said as I sat down across from her in the training room.

"Not like we'd be doing anything else."

That gave her pause. "Did you have something else in mind?"

I sighed. "Nope. Not a thing." I was closing in on the end of the second week of my time with the Unseen, but it felt like a lifetime. Everyone kept telling me I'd accomplished an unimaginable amount of work. Suddenly, I felt like I'd appreciate a break.

"You can have a break on Saturday."

"And I will!" She rolled her eyes at my enthusiasm. "Tracy, can I ask you something?"

"Yes."

I tried to formulate my thoughts into an intelligent question, not wanting to waste her time. "I never see you in the common area after we train. What do you do to unwind?"

"Unwind? I'm afraid I don't understand."

"You're always working, always with your nose to the grindstone. What do you do for fun?" I pressed.

She looked hard at me. "This, Mackenzie. This is what I do for fun. If I take it seriously, it's because I want you to succeed. You have more potential than anyone I've ever seen. That excites me." Her voice remained flat when she said it, but the sparkle in her eye spoke to her genuine passion for her job. "When I'm not training, I'm studying techniques, training methods, and new uses for readers. I'm working hard to stay one step ahead of you, so in the future, I'll still have things to teach you. You possess an extraordinary mind and I, for one, don't intend to waste it."

Okay then, I thought.

"If that's all..." She paused, and I nodded. Even if I had something else to ask her, I knew I wouldn't get a straight answer. "Today, we'll work on keeping readers out."

"What do you mean? I learned how to push unwanted readers out yesterday."

"Yes, and while that is a vital skill, it's best if you can keep them from ever entering your mind in the first place."

That made sense to me.

"These defenses will not only prevent others from entering your mind, but they'll contain your outgoing thoughts too."

I perked up. "So, everyone will stop hearing my thoughts."

"Ideally, yes."

"Ideally indeed," I mused, longing for the return of some privacy. Up until two weeks ago, I'd never had to worry about keeping my thoughts to myself. I was the only reader on my playing field. I didn't like having the tables turned, and I looked forward to the return of some peace. I was pretty sure everyone else was eager for that too.

"I've heard it likened to building a wall around your mind to keep your thoughts in, and others out. That's as basic as I can make it for you."

"I suppose I'll have to figure out the rest?"

"It's worked for you so far."

"I guess it has." I couldn't help the skepticism in my voice. I was new to this. How was I supposed to build a wall in my mind? I sighed. She was right though. I hadn't had much trouble honing my abilities before, so why would this be any different?

And it wasn't. It took me about two days, but I got it. I built my wall with memories, brick by brick. Memories of Maddie, of my aunt, of playing my first instrument, of school, I used everything that made me *me*—the good and the bad—and built the wall higher and higher, until my sanctuary was complete.

It felt different when I was done, sort of warm, like I'd just shut a window against a draft I hadn't realized was coming through. And most importantly, I could tell I was secure.

Thursday afternoon, as I was clearing my dishes from lunch, I caught a glimpse of Mitchell. His skin still had an unhealthy grey tinge to it, but at least he was up and about. He didn't linger, though—he stayed just long enough to nod to Owen and grab some food.

Tracy didn't allow me to dwell on my concern for Mitchell. After my last defensive brick was in place, she gazed at me thoughtfully. "I wonder if you might let me try something."

"As long as it doesn't involve killing me, sure. What's up?" Her wicked smile unnerved me. "Hey, I wasn't kidding."

"I'm not going to hurt you. Just stay behind your wall." She leaned forward, staring intently, making me very uncomfortable.

I retreated as far back as I could get, both in the room and in my mind. Bracing myself for whatever she might give me, I tensed and waited. And waited. And waited. She sat back, sweat beading on her forehead, despite the steady temperature in the room.

A satisfied grin spread across her face. "Very impressive indeed, Mackenzie."

"What?"

"I have just attempted to invade your mind. I tried repeatedly, using several different methods, and nothing worked. Your defenses are already stronger than those of many Unseen."

"Already?"

"Smart readers are always honing their defenses, learning how to fortify them against stronger readers. Their training doesn't stop."

I nodded, wondering just how far I could go with my abilities.

"That is the question of the day, isn't it?"

"More like the question of the month."

She smiled, and it softened her features. Suddenly, she looked like someone I could be friends with, not my hard-as-nails glorified drill instructor. "Yes, well. Tomorrow, we will not be training, so you will get the break you wanted."

"Really? That's awesome. I was thinking of going to see my friend Maddie."

"No, I didn't mean you could shirk your responsibilities to the Unseen. I meant you wouldn't be training with me. Nothing more, nothing less."

I frowned. "So, what am I going to do instead?"

"You will be meeting with David first thing."

My frown deepened. "David? Why?"

"He frequently meets with the trainees to discuss their progress. There's nothing to be worried about." Her attempt at comfort only made me more concerned.

She stood, signaling that we were finished. "One more

thing. Now that you have them, keep your defenses up at all times. Even around Owen. The more you can keep to yourself, the better."

"Oh, don't you worry. They'll be at their strongest around Owen."

The smile returned to her face. "Good girl." Once again, she left before I could respond.

Owen came in before I could collect myself enough to follow Tracy out. "Are you coming?" He paused for a second. "It's very quiet in here."

I decided to play it coy. "Is it?"

His eyes narrowed. "You've blocked me out!" Closing the distance between us, he lifted me off the ground. "That's amazing! Good for you!"

Caught off guard by his reaction, I tried to catch up. "Thanks," I said, lacking his enthusiasm.

"What's wrong?"

"Nothing, I just didn't think you'd be this excited about not knowing every time I swoon over you."

He put me down and smoothed his shirt. "Well, that's true. I am at a disadvantage now."

"I prefer to think of it as leveling the playing field."

He smacked my butt on our way out of the training room. "I'll show you how to level the playing field."

I squealed and ran away, Owen trailing behind me.

Mitchell appeared at the entrance to the stairway, looking a little more human all the time. His skin was slowly getting peachier, and his eyes weren't quite so sunken. He no longer looked like the Grim Reaper was standing over his shoulder, and that was a step in the right direction if you asked me.

He avoided eye contact with me as we approached. We came to a halt in front of him, both of us a little out of breath. "Good to see you up and around, Mitchell," I said.

He nodded, though he was clearly uncomfortable with talking about his excursion.

"How are you feeling?" I asked.

"Fine." His one-word answer was followed by a long silence that stretched awkwardly throughout the gym.

Owen cleared his throat. "Where are you headed?"

"Down to David's office to finish debriefing."

Owen nodded once. "Come find us when you're done. We'll probably be watching a movie or something."

He nodded, and then he turned his gaze to me, almost in spite of himself. A small smile found its way to his mouth. "Hey, I can't hear you." A glint of excitement lit his tired eyes.

"Yup. Tracy's been pushing me hard."

He nodded once, struggling to find the right response. "Well, good work." I could tell the sentiment was genuine, and somehow, it meant more to me than some of the other congratulations I'd received.

"Thanks." I so badly wanted to put him at ease, to know more about him, to be his friend. But I sure as heck didn't know how.

Owen came to our rescue again. "Well, you better get in there. David doesn't like to be kept waiting."

He nodded and walked toward David's office.

"Good luck!" I called after him, but he didn't respond.

We turned and started walking up the stairs. "He seems to be doing better, right?" I asked.

"Yeah, he is."

I looked over at Owen, but he was staring straight ahead. Clearly, I wasn't going to get any more information on the subject.

"So…" I hesitated. I wanted to ask him about my meeting with David tomorrow, but I wasn't sure he'd give me any information. But it was on my mind, so I pressed forward. "I'm supposed to have a meeting with David tomorrow morning instead of training."

"Oh." He didn't hide the surprise in his voice. "I suppose that makes sense. You've hit all the marks you're supposed to hit before having a meeting with David."

"I take it you had a meeting with him too?"

"Yeah, after I learned to defend myself. But I'd been here for months, not weeks."

"Yes, well, you've already established yourself as a slow learner." He playfully shoved me. "Tracy said it was just a status update sort of meeting, but it feels like more than that to me. I'm uneasy about it."

He looked at the steps rather than at me. "There's nothing to be uneasy about." It came out quickly and sort of barbed. I could tell he was hiding something. It was a sensation that had become all too familiar.

I gazed at him from the corner of my eyes. "Clearly."

He shrugged his shoulders. "There isn't. You should quit being suspicious of us all the time. We're not trying to kill you or whatever else you have cooked up in your head."

"If that's true, then why not tell me the big secret you're all hiding? Or is it secrets, plural?"

He looked at me for just a moment, and I thought he might spill right then and there, but instead, he turned and kept walking. By then, we were on the landing for the common room.

I stopped before going in. "Is that what this meeting is about? The secrets? Will I finally get some answers?" I couldn't help but be excited about the chance to finally learn exactly what I'd gotten myself into.

He was halfway into the common room when he turned to close the distance between us. He leaned in close, and for a moment, I thought he might kiss me. He was so close that I could feel his breath on my face.

He didn't close his eyes like he would if he was leaning in for a kiss. Instead, he looked straight at me, his eyes drilling into me as if he could see into my soul. "You might get the answers you're looking for tomorrow, and you might not." His voice was so low I could feel it in my chest. "All I care about is what you do after your meeting."

"What would I do after my meeting?" I knew there was hidden meaning behind his words, and I wanted him to be the one to spell it out for me.

A sad look flashed in his eyes, but he shrugged his shoulders and it was gone. "What else would you do? Spend time with me." He leaned away, grabbed my hand, and pulled me toward the common area. "Now, let's go watch a movie and enjoy our evening."

What on Earth was that about? I wondered. I replayed his words in my head, *You might get the answers you're looking for tomorrow, and you might not. All I care about is what you do after your meeting.* And then there was the way he'd held me so close, almost as if he were afraid he might lose me. *All I care about is what you do after your meeting.* What in God's name could David possibly tell me that would tear Owen and me apart?

It was troubling enough to keep me from concentrating on the movie. I'd been so excited about getting answers that I hadn't thought of the possible consequences of what David might tell me. I'd just assumed he would sing my praises and give me some cushy spot with the Unseen. But what if that wasn't what happened tomorrow? What if he told me something I didn't want to hear?

I frowned and looked to Owen. He might no longer be able to read my thoughts, but he could still read *me*. We both retreated to the library, heading immediately for the piano.

"You can finish the movie if you'd like," I said.

"I'd prefer to sit next to you."

"Suit yourself," I said, losing myself in the music, momentarily banishing my troubles.

That night, when the music was gone, I lay in bed, staring at the ceiling, counting the popcorn pieces that glimmered down at me. I tried to fathom what David could possibly tell me that would make me want to leave. Coming up empty, I rolled over and tried to get some sleep, but I couldn't. Something nagged at the back of my mind. Something Tracy had once said.

A rather deadly asset…
The words floated in my mind as I drifted off to sleep.

18

I had no idea what time I finally drifted off, but when my alarm went off, I wasn't ready. I slapped at it, knocking my phone to the ground. The sound only got louder due to lack of attention, which made my flailing to reach the damn thing more pronounced.

Eventually, I gave in and got out of bed. Retrieving my phone from the floor, I said, "You win this round," and silenced the alarm, which was blasting by then. I was sleeping so deeply, I had trouble bringing the numbers on the clock into focus, let alone comprehend what they meant. Then it all came rushing back to me. David, Owen, Tracy, Mitchell, the Unseen, a deadly asset…

I got up and rushed to the bathroom, attempting to brush my teeth and tame my hair at the same time. There was still plenty of time, but the sooner I got there, the sooner I might get my answers. I might not like what I learned, but I couldn't be in this limbo stage anymore.

Being an adult was about asking questions and making the best you could from the answers you got, which was exactly what I intended to do.

Owen was waiting for me when I pulled up, but we didn't

speak. The air was thick with things unsaid between the two of us. Silence reigned all the way to David's office.

As we stood in front of the boss' door, he stared at me, his eyes pleading. "Good luck," he said.

"Thanks."

We stood face-to-face for a heartbeat. I searched his eyes, wondering what secrets lived behind them and how many would be unlocked for me today.

The desire to have his lips on mine overwhelmed me, and I leaned forward. The small action was all he needed, and he claimed my mouth. His kiss was so passionate. I could tell he feared it might be the last time.

When he finally released me, my head spun, and I took a step back, slightly off balance.

"I hope you find your way back to me."

"I will, Owen." I tried to sound strong and confident, despite my racing heart and mind.

He only nodded in response, and I turned to knock on David's door.

"Yes, come in," he called out.

I watched Owen as I shut the door behind me.

"Hello, Mackenzie. I didn't hear you out there. Very impressive. Please, have a seat." He gestured to the seat across from him.

"So, what have I been called to the principal's office for this time?"

He chuckled. "Nothing bad. This is just a progress report and sort of an informational meeting, as I'm guessing Tracy explained."

"Explained is a loose term for what she did."

"I'm sure you're right," he said through a smile. "Mackenzie, you are the most gifted reader I've ever come across, myself included. Tracy told me what you did with the guide at the caverns. That's very impressive. In fact, it's a skill you should have had to learn. But you just used what you already knew and inferred what to do next. You have the opportunity to take this as far as you'd like. Your abilities will open more doors to you than are available to the rest of us."

"Opportunities like what?"

He continued talking without acknowledging my question. "Never in the history of the organization has someone gone through their training as quickly and skillfully as you. In fact, I've been trying to read you this entire time, and I haven't been able hear a single thought."

He watched as a sly smile played on my face. Of course, I had realized what he was doing. I could feel him trying to chip away at my defenses without any luck.

"Yes. You should be proud of being able to keep the boss out of your head. Less than a handful of the Unseen are capable of that. All of them have been with me for quite some time." He paused. "Well, all of them save for you."

"Perhaps I will just ask you this, since I can't get the information myself. What is your plan moving forward, Mackenzie?"

"My plan?"

"How do you see yourself fitting in here with us?"

Great. An interview question I was entirely unprepared for. Get ready for an epic fail in 3... 2... 1... "I don't really know, to be honest. Everyone has so many secrets. And although Tracy is training me, I'm still very much an outsider. Until I'm truly one of you, I don't have any idea how I can contribute or fit in." There. That was easy enough.

He sat back in his chair. "Mackenzie, do you want to be a member of the Unseen? Would you like to join us?"

Confusion took hold. "I'm sorry; I thought I already had joined you."

He hesitated and brought his folded hands to his mouth, as if searching for the right words. "Mackenzie, I'm going to tell you a story. It's about a young family. The parents aren't much older than you are, and they have two young children, both still in diapers. The parents are rare by today's standards. They love each other very much, and they love their children even more. They spend time with both of them, read to them, nurture them, and fawn over them. But one day, the oldest is killed. He's shot in the backseat of their car while the mother is driving home from the grocery store."

He paused to let the horror of that scenario sink in. "At first, the shooting is deemed an accident. A random act of violence that was the direct result of the family being in the wrong place at the wrong time. A bullet meant for someone else tragically found the two-and-a-half-year-old boy."

Tears threatened my eyes. Why was I getting so emotional? This wasn't true. *Get a hold of yourself.* I cleared my throat and waited for him to continue.

"But as police investigate, it's uncovered that the child was targeted, the shooting was deliberate, and the murder of a toddler had occurred."

"But why?"

"Why is not the correct question."

"So, what is?"

"If you had the power to stop it, to save the child, to keep the family whole, would you do it?"

"I—"

He cut me off. "Before you answer, think about what saving the child might mean. Would you be willing to take a life? To kill the shooter?"

Without thinking, I responded, "Yes. If it would save the child."

"What if the shooter had a family of his own? A child the same age waiting for him to come home? A child who would wait forever because you took his daddy away?"

My head spun. How could I possibly value one life over another? But after a moment, I said, "Perhaps the shooter was a bad influence on the child and removing him from the kid's life was for the best." I couldn't believe I'd said such a thing. I thought about how keenly I'd felt the absence of my own parents, immediately regretting what I'd said. "I don't mean that," I said in a quiet voice. "A child should have their father. No matter what."

A pained expression crossed his face. "Yes, I agree." It was so quiet, I wondered if I'd imagined him saying that.

Silence hung in the room. I didn't know what to say, and David seemed to be struggling for words as well.

Eventually, he broke the silence. "Mackenzie, if you commit to the Unseen, these are the types of situations you will be faced with."

"I'm sorry, what?"

"I realize this must be very shocking to you."

"No, go back to the killing part. You want me to do what to who?"

"Maybe I should start over. The Unseen is a counterterrorist group working with the government."

"What exactly does that mean? You're murderers who are excused for your crimes?"

"No, we're not murderers."

"I'm sorry, do you kill people or not?" My anger was building. They'd all lied to me, from start to finish. Every last one of them.

"Well, yes, but we also save hundreds and thousands of lives every year with the work we do."

The tears I'd held back earlier spilled over. I'd never been betrayed like this before. These people knew everything about me, and the fact that I had been wrong to trust them slapped me in the face so hard it stung. "You're the one who just got done telling me that everyone has a family. Everyone is a son, brother, father, husband. Why the hell would you tell me that if you're trying to get me to be some sort of assassin?"

"Because you need to be able to face this from all the different angles. You must make your final decision knowing exactly what you're getting into."

I got to my feet, glaring at him. "I am *not* a killer. And you were wrong to think I ever could be." I stormed out of his office, tears flowing freely.

19

Owen was waiting for me, and he rushed to catch up to me when I flew past him without pausing. "Mackenzie, wait."

"I do not wait for murderers," I said, giving him my back as I climbed the stairs two at a time. I had to get out of there. I needed away from these people.

"Please, let me explain."

I turned to him. "Who are you?" Right there in the staircase, I demanded the answers I'd been waiting for so patiently.

"What?"

Wrong answer, I thought, and turned my back on him, pressing on toward the ground floor.

"Mackenzie, please, I don't understand your question."

Rather than look at him, I continued moving. *If I can just get back to the light of day, maybe this will all be a bad dream.* "You know damn well what I'm asking you." I burst through the front door, squinting at the brightness of the morning sun. But Owen was still behind me.

"I can't read you anymore. I really *don't* understand. Please, let's talk about this. Don't leave this way. Let me try to explain."

"What do you have to explain to me if you don't understand what I'm asking?" I turned to face the first and only man to break my heart. My impatience for his secrets had dried my tears.

He looked at me, his hands held out to me in surrender, but he said nothing.

"Did you just act like you had feelings for me to get me to join the group? Was I your assignment? Acquire the exceptional reader?"

Horror filled his face, but I felt like it was an act, all of it. I couldn't trust any of them. "No! That wasn't it at all." He reached for me, but I pulled away. "Mackenzie, I care very much for you."

I eyed him with suspicion. "Fine. Then tell me the truth. How many people have you killed?"

He sighed. "Maybe we should focus on how many people I've saved."

"How many people have you killed?" I demanded again.

He didn't answer at first, so I was surprised when he eventually spoke. "Four," he said after what seemed like an eternity. "So far," he added.

Horror made me retch right then and there, losing everything I'd eaten in the last few hours on to the pavement. I wiped my mouth. *Four people. He'd taken four different lives.*

"I trusted you. I thought you were different. Someone who could be a real partner. But you turned out to be the worst one of all. You're a—" I choked on the word, "—murderer." I whipped around, hoping I'd smacked him in the face with my ponytail.

I crossed the parking lot in record speed while he jogged after me. "Mackenzie, please. Consider the consequences before you leave this way."

"Are you threatening me?"

"No! But there are other dangers."

"What dangers?" I looked at him, seeing a cold, hard killer instead of the man I'd grown to care about. Where my body had once been drawn to him, it was now violently repelled. He disgusted me. I needed to get away. "You know what? It doesn't matter. I was fine without you before, and I will be again."

I tried to open my car door, but Owen grabbed my arm. "Mackenzie," he said, looking deep into my eyes. A flash of the old desire bubbled up, but the leftover bile in the back of my throat didn't make it hard to push it back down.

I tried to free my arm, but he held fast. "I care about you. I don't want anything to happen to you."

"Oh, yeah? Like what? Like I could be a totally normal person who never kills anyone or commits a crime of any kind for her whole life?" I spat. "Sure, I'll probably die a lonely old maid, but at least my conscience will be clear."

He looked at me in that special way he had, where he seemed to be seeing into my very soul. "You may not live long enough to become an old maid."

I glared at him. He was just trying to manipulate me into staying by using scare tactics, or at least that was what I told myself. The look in his eyes said he was telling the truth, but how could I trust him after everything he'd kept from me?

"You want answers? Stay long enough to hear me out, and I'll give them to you."

My car keys jangled in my hand as I debated what to do. Even now, I didn't want to lose Owen. But I also didn't want him to be a killer, and I certainly didn't want to join him down that path. "You've had plenty of chances to tell me your secrets."

He had no defense, but at least he didn't look away.

I sighed. What could it hurt to listen to him? "Fine. You have ten minutes, and then I'm out of here."

"Do you want to go back inside, where it's a little more comfortable?"

I leaned against my car. "I'm as comfortable as I'm going to get. Nine minutes, thirty seconds."

"You know, I wasn't alone like you were. My whole family could read minds."

He's finally telling me a little more about his family? I tightened my hands into fists, refusing to get sucked into his story this easily.

"We were like peas in a pod. My little brother was annoying at times, but I still loved him, the way brothers do. My folks were great at teaching us about our abilities, helping us get through our awkward childhoods with this extra little complication. They didn't tell us how to control it or anything, not like the Unseen do, but they helped us cope, told us what was normal, what to expect in public, stuff like that."

"Must've been nice," I said, with more bitterness in my voice than I'd intended to show.

He smiled warmly, thinking about his family. "It *was* nice, for a time... then they were taken away from me one by one. My brother was the first to go. They said it was a rare form of cancer. A quick and silent killer, they called it. One day, he was fine; the next, he was gone." He paused, a deep frown creasing his face.

Despite my anger toward him in that moment, my heart went out to him. I didn't have any siblings, but I imagined it was immeasurably difficult to lose one.

"How old were you?"

"Hmm?" He looked at me like he'd forgotten I was there for a moment. "Oh, I was twelve. Jason was ten. My parents were destroyed, as you can imagine, but we soldiered on, clinging to each other for support. Some days, that's all we did—hold each other up until it was time to go to bed, then start over again the next day. It was horrible. I didn't think it could get any worse, but then it did."

"My mom usually took me to school, but she had an early meeting one day, so Dad took me. If she'd driven me, maybe she wouldn't have gotten into the accident. Or I guess I could have been killed with her. It's hard to say."

"Well, you can't blame yourself. It was just an accident."

He smiled, though this time the expression was bitter. "Yes, that's exactly what I was told. It was just an accident. Unpreventable. Tragic. I heard a lot of those words. In less than a year, half of my family was taken from me. The worst part of it was that my mom was the best one of us. She loved without question, which I find to be a rare quality in people." He shrugged. "Maybe that's why I care for you so much. You accepted me even though I couldn't answer your questions."

Just how deep did his feelings go? My knees nearly gave way. It was too much. I opened my car door and sat down in the driver's seat.

Owen continued his story without commenting on my movement. "The last person to go was my dad. They said he fell onto the train tracks. Another 'tragic' accident. It had been just over a year since Jason, just over a year since my family was whole."

He looked off into the distance, squinting into the sun. "After that, I bounced around in the foster care system for a few months until David found me. He pulled some strings and brought me here, gave me a home. Eventually, he told me the truth."

"What truth? That they're all murderers?"

"No, that my family had been killed one by one by the enemy—a group trained to eliminate other readers. He'd worked hard to find me before the enemy could. The disorganization of the foster care system is probably what saved my life."

It echoed of David's story about the little boy who'd been shot. I looked at him skeptically. Was this the truth or another lure? "And you just took his word for it?"

"No, I didn't. I was still reeling from losing my whole family. I couldn't get my mind around some elaborate conspiracy theory. It just seemed too unlikely. But I also didn't have anywhere else to go, so I hung around and heard him out. He showed me the evidence they had against these people."

"These people?"

"The ones who'd hunted my family down. Even my ten-year-old brother. How much of a threat could he have been? They killed him anyway. They said it was a mercy to kill him first." A hatred I'd never seen before clouded his eyes. "They weren't even sorry."

My emotions warred with themselves. "Sounds like you weren't very sorry about the four people you killed."

"No, I suppose I'm not. Three of the four were kill-or-be-killed scenarios, and I chose my own life over theirs. If that's selfish, fine. But don't judge me too harshly until you've looked down the barrel of a gun."

"And the fourth?"

"The fourth was—" he hesitated, "—difficult. He was unassuming, and he actually seemed like a nice guy on the surface. I questioned David more than once, since I wanted to make sure we had the right guy. He just didn't seem like he had it in him. Long story short, I got my hands on some direct evidence linking him to a plot to release a massively deadly airborne virus at the Olympics that year. It would have killed at least ten thousand people. In the end, I chose to take one life in order to save many."

I tried to get my head around it. Everything he was saying made sense. It was reasonable. Certainly, I wouldn't expect him to stand there and be killed if someone was threatening him. The fourth man's death was a little harder to rationalize, but if what he said was true, he had saved a staggering amount of people.

He reached for my hand, pulling me out of my internal debate. "Mackenzie. The bottom line is, there are truly bad people out there, and the Unseen aren't them."

I looked at his hand holding mine. It was big, and it covered my entire hand, making me feel encompassed by him. Protected. "Enemy is a dangerous word to use flippantly. I imagine the mothers who are without their children find you to be the enemy, don't you think?"

He opened his mouth to answer, but I kept talking. "And what about the wives without their husbands? You're their enemy too. And those children who have to grow up without a father or mother…" I shook my head. "No matter how you slice it, it's still killing." I shook loose from his hand. "I'm sorry, Owen, I truly am, but I just can't do this…"

Before I could see the expression on his face, I got the rest of the way into my car, shut the door, and drove away, not once looking back to see Owen—and the Unseen—disappear from my life forever.

20

Despite the fact that it was a four-hour drive, I barely even registered the length of the trip to Maddie's.

I've never felt this betrayed, I thought over and over and over again. Owen's face flashed through my mind, and regret stabbed me in the gut. But I thought again of those families David had mentioned, the families of the "enemy," as it were. But maybe I was thinking about this the wrong way. Enemy was such a loaded word—replace "enemy" with "danger" and maybe the Unseen's mission was more palatable. Owen said he'd killed four people, three of whom were a direct threat to him. They were all a danger that needed to be eliminated. The fourth was a danger to thousands of others, although not a direct danger to him.

I shook my head, trying to recapture the anger I'd initially felt. *Now you're rationalizing killing*, I told myself, *justifying it even. This isn't a Bourne movie. This is real life. And real death.* But what would I do if someone held a gun to my face? Would I try to protect myself? I had no idea. Despite the fact that I hadn't had an easy road, it hadn't exactly been that difficult either. I'd never faced death, and I intended to keep it that way for as long as possible.

Owen's voice echoed in my mind. *You may not live to be an old maid.*

The story of his family played like a movie on fast-forward in my head. I knew he was trying to show me that some readers weren't safe when they stood alone. It occurred to me that he might have made the story up to convince me to stay, but something about it held an element of truth. And that look in his eyes…

Despite having spent the entire drive thinking through every angle of my situation, I didn't feel any better by the time I pulled into the parking spot in front of Maddie's apartment. I don't know how long I sat there, staring blankly ahead, but Maddie snapped me out of it when she knocked on my window.

"This is a nice surprise!" Her muffled voice floated through the closed window. Her expression changed when she saw my face. She shifted her bags to one hand and opened my car door. "I was just coming home from the store. Mac, what happened? Did that bastard break your heart?" When I didn't answer right away, she retracted her statement. "If he didn't, I take back the bastard comment."

I stared straight ahead, my hands still on the steering wheel. "They lied to me, Maddie. All of them."

"Who?"

"The Unseen."

"The what?"

I wasn't loyal to them anymore, was I? How much could I tell her? None of it, if I still didn't want her to know I was a mind reader. All of it, if I finally wanted to share my secret with the one person in the whole world I could trust without hesitation.

While I debated, Maddie frowned. "All right, why don't you come inside and tell me what happened from the beginning?"

She must have helped me out of the car and into her apartment, because the next thing I knew, I was sitting on her couch with a mug of tea between my hands.

She stared at me expectantly, showing more patience than I've ever seen from her. I expected her to start yelling, 'Spit it out already!' I was sure she wanted to, but she didn't. I looked at her then, and it dawned on me that for the first time in our long friendship, I didn't have my iLs and I wasn't hearing her thoughts.

At least I'd gotten some control out of this mess, I thought.

I took a deep breath. "Honestly, I'm not sure how much I can tell you."

She nodded but waited patiently.

"Things started out great. They taught me to live without my iLs."

"Wow. I haven't seen you in public without it since we were kids. How did they do that?"

"It was part of the training. I had to learn to be without it."

"Jesus, Mac, you didn't tell me any of that! Was it hard?"

"At first, but I caught on a lot quicker than any of the therapists who treated me when I was a kid would've believed." The tea she gave me was warm and calming as it slid down my throat.

"Okay, so they taught you to live without your iLs. Sounds good to me. When did things go south?"

"Today."

"Right. I figured as much since you showed up like a zombie at my door, after not getting more than an occasional text from you for like five days."

I just looked at her, not really processing her comment or her sarcasm.

"Okay, something is really wrong here, and I'm just trying to get my head around it." Panic was replacing frustration in her voice. "So what happened? Did the hot guy cheat on you? I'll kill him if you didn't already."

"No, Owen didn't cheat on me."

Confusion played across her face. "I don't understand…"

177

"They lied to me." *They're killers.* It was on the tip of my tongue, ready to spill out, but something held the words back, perhaps the instinct that once said, they could never be unsaid.

"Lied to you about what?"

There it was. The question I wasn't prepared to answer.

Tears pooled in my eyes when I looked at her, and she was by my side in an instant, her arms around me. "Mac, you know I'm only good at tough love."

I looked at her while the tears spilled down my cheeks.

"Why did you come here? If you want my help, you have to tell me what you need from me."

"I came here because you're the only family I have. The only person I trust in the whole world." It wasn't a lie, so why was I hesitating to tell her my secret? *She's right; she can only help me if she knows what happened.*

"Maddie, throughout our entire friendship, I've been keeping something from you."

Her eyes narrowed. "I *knew* you took that Barbie. I *knew* it! Mac, it's not a big deal. We were like five. It's certainly not something to be blubbering about more than twenty years later."

I stared at her, wondering if she could possibly be ready to hear what I had to say. It was too late, though. I'd set the ball in motion, and there was no stopping it now. "I'm a mind reader."

She laughed at first, but the sound cut off abruptly when she realized I was serious. "You mean your Spidey sense?"

"My Spidey sense is reading minds."

A new wave of panic spread across her face and she swallowed hard, having a hard time coming up with a response.

Reaching out for her mind, I read her thoughts purposefully for the first time.

Holy shit, she's lost it. She's gone totally crazy. What can I do for her? Should I take her to a hospital?

"I'm not crazy, Maddie."

"No, of course not. No one said you are." She turned away from me a little bit. "I just need a moment to process this."

Think faster. She knows I think she's lost it. I had an aunt who was institutionalized. Maybe I should call my mom. She might know what to do.

"I don't think your mom will be able to help. I'm pretty sure my case is different from your aunt's. Also, the less people who know my secret, the better."

"I..." She trailed off.

Did I say any of that out loud?

"No, you didn't."

"Stop. Just let me think for a second."

I knew exactly how she felt, after having the Unseen inside my head for so long.

Thirty-nine.

"Thirty-nine."

Holy shit.

"Holy shit."

She sat back on the couch, her eyes wide.

"The iLs helped me to block out other people's thoughts so I could concentrate."

"The first day of school..." she said, trailing off.

"Yeah, that was a hard day for me. There were so many voices, and nowhere for me to hide from them." I sipped my tea, letting that sink in before I went on. "The Unseen, the people I was working for, are readers like me. Until they approached me, I had no idea there were others. I thought I was all alone... a freak. Discovering them was like a dream come true, a dream I'd never dared to entertain. They taught me how to control my gift, how to choose whose voice I wanted to hear and whose I didn't, even how to protect my mind from other readers."

"That all sounds totally bizarre, but great. What went wrong?" She shook her head. I couldn't believe how well she was taking all of this, and I was so relieved to finally level with her.

"I was flying through my training. Things that took everyone else months or even years took me two weeks. So, they let me in on their KFC secret recipe."

"Uh huh…"

I struggled with what to say next, but really, there was only one way to say it. "Turns out they're a bunch of government assassins. They kill terrorists and potential threats to society. And they wanted me to become one of them."

"Holy shit." She said it quietly.

"Yes. I've been hearing that a lot lately."

"This is huge." She paused, taking a moment to formulate a response. "You mean… you have the opportunity to stop things like 9-11 from happening?"

Her tone confused me. She was *excited* by the Unseen's mission. "Maddie, they're killers." There. I had said it.

"I don't understand."

"*I* don't understand," I echoed.

"You have the chance to save lives—"

I cut her off. "By taking lives, Maddie. I'm not a killer, and I don't ever intend to become one."

She stared at me, chewing on her bottom lip. "Are you reading my thoughts right now?"

"No. I didn't think it was appropriate."

"Good call." She took a breath. "So, what happened with Owen?"

"He told me this horrible story about how his whole family was killed by terrorists, and he was rescued by the boss guy, David. I'm hoping it was a lie to get me to stay."

"Jeez, Mac. What if it wasn't?"

I just looked at her, unable to hide the pain I felt from leaving Owen and the Unseen behind.

"Seriously. Why would he lie to you about that? Really?"

"Maybe so I would stay and be their quote 'deadly

asset' end quote."

Her face remained neutral while she mentally chewed on that. "That's kind of intense."

"Intense wasn't the word I'd use. Ridiculous? Idiotic? Those are more fitting, I think."

"What makes you think you couldn't be a deadly asset?"

"It's not that I couldn't... I *wouldn't*. I wouldn't kill someone, Maddie. Maybe if I was in a life-or-death situation, a fight instinct would kick in, but why insert myself into something like that?"

"Mac, there's no question whether or not your fight instinct would kick in. It already has."

"What?"

"With your charming attempted rapist date?"

I groaned. "I totally forgot about him. So much has happened in the last month."

Leaning back on the couch, she sighed and looked up at the clock. "It's late."

I couldn't quite comprehend how it was already dark outside, let alone how it was 2:00 am.

"I have to level with you," Maddie said after a moment. "I think you're making a mistake. These people have the potential to make a real positive change in this country, which means *you* have the potential to make a positive change. And you can save people's lives. That's amazing. Why wouldn't you want to be a part of that? Remember? 'With great power, comes great responsibility.' "

"I'm not a killer, Maddie."

"You said that." She yawned and stood up. "But are you a savior?"

21

Morning came much too quickly after our late-night chatting marathon. Maddie had a workshop first thing, so she was up and around, neither bright eyed nor bushy tailed.

"I can drop you off if you want," I offered from my spot on the couch, rubbing my eyes.

"Nah. I have some prep reading I want to get done, and the train is a good place for that."

I felt bad making her ride the train when I could easily give her a ride. "I have no problem dropping you off."

"I know. Why don't you just hang out here? I'll be done by three. We can get some dinner downtown if you'd like."

"That's all right. I should get back anyway. Start looking for other work. Maybe get in touch with Shelly Goldstein."

"Who?"

"The woman with the dream job."

She frowned. "You'd rather work with troubled kids than save lives?"

"Who says that wouldn't be saving lives?"

She shrugged. "Point taken, I suppose." She came

over and hugged me. "Just think about it, before you do anything too rash."

"Rash thing already done. I left."

"Maybe. Maybe it's not as final as you think. If you want to go back, I'm willing to bet they'd take you."

"Maddie, I'm not going back. I'm not going to kill people for a living."

"Boy, I would." She gave me a devilish smile.

I laughed. "I know you would."

"Lock up when you leave. I'll see you soon, okay?"

"Okay. Have fun at the workshop. Why a Saturday workshop? That's dumb, by the way."

She was half out the door. "I know, but it's supposed to be really good, about how to incorporate technology into your classroom with the Promethean Board. I'm actually excited about it."

"Ugh, go! You exhaust me!"

"I wasn't the one who kept us up until two am talking. Just sayin'."

I laughed, and she shut the door behind her. I wasn't far behind her. I hadn't brought anything with me, not even a toothbrush. I just got up, folded the blanket she'd given me, left a thank-you note on the fridge saying how amazing she was, and headed home.

The drive felt much longer than it had on the way down. The last thing I'd expected was for Maddie to disagree with my decision. I thought she'd be just as horrified as I was. Truth was, her reaction had me questioning my decision.

Could I be a savior? It certainly was a romantic way of looking at it.

Something tickled at the back of my mind. *Is Maddie right?* Either way, it felt like a dangerous game to play. I thought about what happened to Mitchell, and wondered what series of events had led to his injury, whether the mission had been successful, and if he believed risking his life had been worth it. Judging from his post-recovery attitude, he'd probably say it had been. The Unseen believed in their cause. The question was, did I?

It was early afternoon by the time I got home. I grabbed a snack, my laptop, and the remote, settling onto the couch. I flipped on the news, intending to draft an email to Shelly with the newscasters as background noise, but a word caught my ear.

"—on the new Sun Rail commuter train. So far, the death toll is estimated at ten people, but more bodies are being uncovered as we speak."

My mouth went dry. It *couldn't* have been her train.

"So far, no suspects have been named in the bombing, and authorities believe the person responsible may have been killed on board."

A bombing? On the Sun Rail? That makes no sense. The Sun Rail didn't carry enough people to be an effective target. Why not bomb the subway in New York? Why the Sun Rail? I scanned the ticker tape running along the bottom of the screen, searching for information that would confirm Maddie was safe.

Reaching for my phone, I dialed Maddie without taking my eyes off the screen. The wreckage was a tangled mess. You couldn't even tell it had been a train, except for a single semi-intact car at the edge of the frame. My heart began to race as the phone rang and rang. Maddie always picked up on the first or second ring when she was available.

"Hey, it's Maddie, leave me a message and if it's important, I'll call you back."

"Hey, I heard about the train. Just wanted to make sure you're okay. Call me." I hung up, feeling sick. *She was at the workshop all day. It wasn't her train.*

An urgent knock at my door startled me out of my thoughts.

I opened the door absently, still not taking my eyes off the TV.

Owen pushed me back into my apartment.

"Wha—?" I stumbled over my own two feet .

"We have to go. You're not safe here."

"What are you talking about?"

"I'll explain in the car. Grab what you need; you're not coming back here."

"Whoa. You don't get to tell me what I'm doing. Slow down, tell me what's going on, and *maybe* I'll think about coming with you."

He turned his attention to the TV. The reporter was repeating the details while they played footage of the scene of the bombing in the background.

"They're sending a message." The look he gave me sent chills all the way down to my toes. "You're next, Mackenzie."

"I... what? Are you implying this was directed at me? How?"

His eyes turned sad. "It was Maddie's train."

"No," I whispered. "*No!* You can't possibly know that. How do you know that?"

"We know. And we also know that you're not safe. Not here. Not now. You need to come with me."

I collapsed to the ground, unhearing. The TV, Owen, the apartment, all of it melted away, until it was just me, alone. Completely alone. Forever. Maddie was my rock, my partner in crime, my family, my everything. How could she be gone? If she was, I had only myself to blame. I'd led them right to her.

Owen was rustling around, but I paid no attention.

It wasn't her train. It couldn't have been. There was some mistake. She hadn't answered her phone because the workshop was running a little long, that was all. She'd call me back or text me any minute. I clutched my phone in my hand so tightly my fingers turned white. I willed this last lifeline to ring, chime, anything that would prove Maddie hadn't been on that train.

Owen hoisted me up into his arms. "What are you doing?"

"We're leaving. You're not safe." He grunted a little as he pulled the door shut behind him.

"But—"

"No buts. Boss' orders. We're out of here."

But why would David care about my safety after the way I'd told him off and stormed out of the building yesterday? I sagged against Owen's chest. I couldn't take all of this.

He plopped me down in the passenger's seat of his car, circling around to toss something into the trunk. It felt like everything around me was on fast forward, while I was stuck in slow motion.

Memories of Maddie overwhelmed me. Late-night talks about boys. Maddie's smiling face in the crowd at my first concert. Her tears over her first broken heart. Her next crush a few weeks later. The memories kept coming, fast and furious. My lie of omission had stood between us for years, but other than that, we'd had the perfect friendship—more open and honest than anyone could hope for. Maddie was the best person I'd ever known. How could someone like that be taken from a world that needed her so badly?

Tears streamed freely down my face while Owen rummaged around in the trunk of the car. Before I knew it, he was beside me and we were speeding off toward the Unseen.

22

Somewhere between my apartment and the Unseen's facility, my brain started to click into gear.

"Tell me what you think happened," I demanded, still clutching my phone, desperate to hear it ring.

"We think the Potestas found out about you, although we're not sure how." He paused, making a sharp turn. "One thing's for sure; they'll eventually come after you."

"I'm sorry, the Potestas?"

"For lack of a better word, they're the enemy, the main group of terrorists we're fighting."

"The enemy," I repeated. *That word again.* I sucked in a breath through my teeth, like the phrase had burned me.

"Assuming that's true, and I'm not saying it is, because I can't believe Maddie was on that train, why not stop what happened if you already knew all this information?"

"The information is streaming in quickly now, but it's after the fact." He chanced a sideways glance at me. "I know that doesn't help you much now."

"Or Maddie," I mumbled.

He pulled into the garage behind the Unseen's building. Just as he was reaching for the key, the DJ cut off the music. "Sorry to interrupt folks, but we just got a disturbing piece of information about the Sun Rail bombing. Police are beginning to release the identities of those killed on the train."

"Mac, we should—"

"Shh!" I cut him off.

"A mother of two, a construction worker, and a local teacher are among the dead. Our prayers go out to the families of the victims." The music started up again, but I didn't hear it. All I heard was *a local teacher*.

A local teacher. I looked over at Owen, pleading with him. "It wasn't her. Right?"

From the look on his face, I could tell his heart was breaking for me right then and there in the car.

"Mackenzie…"

"Oh, God," I whispered. Shock was the only thing keeping my tears at bay.

Owen softly placed a hand on my shoulder. "We should go inside. David is waiting. I know he's anxious to see you."

I looked at his hand on my body like it was poisonous. "Let him wait," I said, my voice low and dangerous.

Owen slowly removed his hand, still staring at me.

"Who the fuck cares about David?" I railed, my voice getting louder with each word. "The center has fallen out of my world. David is nothing to me." The words unstopped my tears, and they flowed freely down my cheeks.

Owen's gaze wasn't on me, though, it was looking just over my shoulder. I turned to see David standing at the window.

23

He didn't knock on the window or do anything courteous. He flung the door open, reached over me to undo my seatbelt, and grabbed my arm roughly, hoisting me out of the car. "Let's go."

I wasn't sure if his harsh tone because of what I'd just said, or if something else was bothering him. Instinct told me it was something else, but I didn't know what.

He kept his hold on my bicep all the way down to his office. Owen followed close behind. Once we were on the bottom floor, David pushed me into his office and turned to lock the door behind Owen.

"What the hell is going on? I don't need you to rough me up like some thug, thank you very much," I said, my grief turning to anger in a flash.

"Where are we at?" Owen asked.

"It's hard to say. The information I'm getting from our agents on the other side is sketchy at best. Obviously, they know about her and her skills."

"Hey, I'm sitting right here," I said, but they continued to ignore me.

"We believe they're sending a message, although I'm not exactly sure if they're trying to scare Mackenzie by killing her friend, or if they're hoping to attack her while she's in shock. More information is needed."

"Okay, you know what," I said, "you two need to start talking to me, or I'm out of here. Cooperation over."

"Ha, if this is your idea of cooperation, I'd like to see you act belligerent," Owen said, biting down on his bottom lip.

"Owen, why don't you make sure the facility is secure? I'll get Mackenzie up to speed."

Disappointment clouded his eyes as he looked between the two of us. He clearly wanted to stay. Well, if he wanted me to beg him not to leave, he'd be standing there forever.

When David locked the door behind Owen, I launched into my attack. "Time to give me some answers."

"I'll tell you everything I know."

"Why Maddie?" My voice shook when I said her name.

"As I said, I need more information to determine the exact reason why your friend was targeted. Like I said, I believe the Potestas were sending you a message. They know who you are, they know what you can do... and they know how to get to you."

"What am I supposed to glean from that? Who cares if they know all that?"

"I care."

"Why?"

"Because it makes you vulnerable, a target." He looked deep into my eyes. "You are too valuable to be taken from me."

I missed a beat. *Did he say from me, or from us?* I decided to ignore it. "I don't understand. I left the Unseen. I'm not valuable to anyone."

"I don't think they knew you left. Otherwise, they might have tried to kill you rather than targeting your friend."

The thought gave me pause. Had I been that close to

190

losing my own life? I swallowed hard. "So does that mean I traded my life for Maddie's?" The thought nearly choked me.

"Don't think about it that way. They had a plan in motion before you ever left the Unseen."

"If that's true, why didn't you stop it?" I was getting louder with each word, but I decided I didn't care. Someone needed to be held accountable, and David was the one in front of me.

His expression turned sad. "I didn't know about it until after. I had Owen follow you when you left to make sure you stayed safe. When you got to Maddie's without a problem, I summoned him back here. I was worried when I heard the news. For a while, I thought you might have been on that train too."

"Why do you care so much about me? Is it just because of my talent? That I'm a prodigy?"

"No. It's because of how valuable you are."

"You said that before. I've only been here for a couple of weeks. Explain my value like I'm a two-year-old."

Sighing, he opened a drawer in his desk. He looked down inside it while he spoke. "Mackenzie, do you know my position with the Unseen?"

"Um…" I hadn't exactly been expecting that comment, so I scrambled to come up with something intelligent, failing miserably.

"Let's just say I'm very high up. I answer only to the head of Homeland Security, and of course, the President, but that's rare."

I gulped. "I assumed this was just a small satellite group of a larger, nationwide organization."

"It is. I specifically requested this station." I didn't have time to wonder why. "Because of my position, my family is extremely vulnerable, and the Potestas are constantly searching for them. I spend much of my time keeping them hidden."

"I… you have a family?" I blurted it out before I

could think of making it more tactful.

"I do." He pulled out what was in his drawer, looking at it lovingly. It appeared to be a picture frame. "My wife…" He paused, pain etched on his face. "My wife was killed by the Potestas. But my daughter has recently come back into my life. And I'm not willing to let her go for a second time."

He turned the frame around, revealing an image of a baby. The image took my breath away once I realized the baby was me.

24

I gasped. A bit dramatic, I know, but I couldn't help it. Of all the things he could have had tucked in that drawer, a picture of me was about the last thing I expected him to pull out. I didn't have any memories of my dad. I'd always been told that both of my parents had died when I was an infant. How could this man in front of me be my father?

The world spun around me, and I sat back in the chair, resting my head on one hand. "This is all too much. I lost my only real family on that train today."

"I'm happy to tell you that isn't true."

I perked up. "Maddie survived?"

He frowned. "No. I meant that you didn't lose your only family."

The way he'd always treated me like I was a special case—and not just because of my talents—started to make sense. But my distrust of him and the Unseen was still fresh. "How do I know you're not lying? As far as I know, my parents died decades ago. Do you think you'll get some kind of promotion or kick back if everyone thinks you're the father of the 'prodigy'? Why would you screw with someone like this?" Tears threatened. I felt like I was drowning in lies, and all I wanted was something true to hold on to.

He took a deep breath, and just like that, he let down his defenses. A barrage of images flooded my mind. In them, I recognized my mother's face—she looked just like she did in the one picture I had of her, but so much lovelier. She had wild, dark hair, just like mine, but her skin was lighter, almost porcelain. Her eyes were positively bewitching, dark blue with flecks of green. I could immediately feel his attraction to her. Memories of their wedding flashed through our connection next. It was a small but beautiful affair in a small church I didn't recognize. There were stained glass rainbows on the floor, and Mom's dress was made of antique lace. She looked lovely as she walked down the aisle toward my dad. His feelings for her overwhelmed me, and I couldn't help but smile. She smiled back, and the expression transformed her into something straight out of a glamor magazine.

The next flash was brief. Mom was pregnant. Dad rested his hand on her huge belly while they both looked at it in a full-length mirror in their bedroom.

Then I was being placed in my dad's arms for the first time. Wiggling and crying, clearly displeased, I fussed and searched for my mother with my mouth.

Last was a funeral.

The pain was crushing. It sucked the air from my lungs. He'd told her family and friends a lie—she'd been killed in a car accident. He convinced himself it wasn't that much of a stretch. She had been killed in a crash, but it was no accident. The Potestas had targeted her to get to him. He was becoming too powerful, too high up with the Unseen. His daughter was next.

The image of me in a bassinet in the corner of the living room surrounded by people in black flashed through my mind, followed by a feeling of resolve.

Then I was left alone in my mind once again. I put my face in my hands, letting the revelations of the last few hours crush me. I couldn't breathe. The room was spinning around me. I gasped for air.

"Mackenzie?" he asked, but his voice seemed far away.

When I woke up, he was holding me, brushing the hair away from my face. "Are you okay?" he asked.

"I am the furthest thing from okay," I said, sitting up slowly.

He offered me a glass of water. I took a sip, and the cold liquid snaked deliciously down my throat. He helped me back into the chair and leaned on his desk, facing me.

"I failed your mother, Mackenzie. I couldn't fail you too," he said as he stared at another picture he'd pulled out, this one of my mother.

"So why not take me with you? Raise me here at the facility? Anything but leave me with her sister. She never loved me... not for one minute."

"She isn't your aunt."

"She... what?"

"She's a member of the Unseen. Trained to keep you safe and hidden."

He said it like it was nothing more than a fact. Like throwing one more little tidbit out there didn't totally change my life and who I was.

"I was an assignment for her?"

"Yes."

I thought for a moment about the woman who had raised me—the closest thing to a mother I'd ever had. Her thoughts had always been very short and to the point, and suddenly, it started to make sense. "She knew I was a reader, didn't she? She guarded her thoughts against me. But not so much that I would suspect something."

"Yes."

"Why did she let me just muddle through? Why not help me deal with it?"

"We decided it wasn't safe for you to know about the Unseen. We tried to keep you as uninformed as possible, since it was the best way to keep the Potestas in the dark as well."

"But she was so horrible to me. Right before I left for

school, she told me I'd stolen her life from her."

He sat back in his chair and rubbed the bridge of his nose. "I'd hoped over time she would soften to you." He sighed. "To her, you did steal her life. She was a very gifted member of the Unseen. She thought she would go far with our organization and imagined a life spent pursuing and eliminating terrorists. When she learned she was to be a single mom for the rest of her life, she wasn't too pleased. She couldn't see the big picture."

I exhaled, as if all the lies that made up my life were leaving my body, making room for the truth. "But that wasn't my fault. I didn't choose her." I looked at him, hurt in my eyes. "You chose her, didn't you? There wasn't anyone better? Perhaps someone with an ounce of kindness to their name? You thought it was better for me to be raised by some heartless bitch?"

My own hurt reflected back at me in his expression. "Believe me, Mackenzie, it's not a choice I took lightly. She was incredibly gifted, and I knew she would keep you safe. After your mom was taken from me so brutally, that was my priority."

I knew how grief-stricken he'd been after experiencing the memories he'd shared with me. "But if they found Mom, they would've known about me. How exactly did you make me disappear in their eyes?"

He didn't look at me. Instead, he reached behind him and pushed a newspaper clipping into my hands. It was the front page of the *Tallahassee Democrat*, dated over twenty-five years ago. The main headline read—*Grief blamed for murder suicide*. The subhead read—*Local man kills infant daughter, then self.*

"Oh my God." It was all I could say. He'd made everyone—their friends, their family—think he'd killed me and then himself. He'd given up his life as he knew it. For me.

"I've killed a fair number of people in my time with the Unseen, more than anyone else in this office. But fabricating your death at my hands was one of the most difficult things I've ever done."

I was at a total loss for words. Everything I knew—or thought I knew—had been turned upside down in one day.

"Of course, the Potestas found out that I was still alive soon enough." He retrieved the newspaper and put it back on his desk behind him, out of sight. "That's when the hunt started for you. And it's never stopped."

"And now they've found me?"

"And now they've found you."

Confusion clouded my mind as I tried to digest everything. "Why did you come to me now? I was happy. I had a plan for my life, even a job offer. But you've turned all of that upside down. For what?"

"Actually, it was an accident. I intended to keep you hidden indefinitely. In the event that I died, someone else would take over for me, but I was determined that no one else would ever learn about you. But when you met Mitchell in the park that day, he told me how desperate you were to meet other readers. And Owen confirmed it for me after watching you that day at the bar. But you already knew that much at least." He sighed heavily.

"So that part was true." He nodded and waited for me to digest everything.

"Honestly, Mac, I would've preferred to keep you safe from this world. You seemed happy, like you had purpose and direction. But when Mitchell told me about seeing you, the temptation was too great for me to ignore. If that was wrong, I apologize."

I laughed a bit maniacally. "So, now I've got a band of killers after me as a result of the world's worst first date." Tears suddenly sprang to my eyes. "But they killed Maddie instead of me. And I led them right to her."

He reached out for my hand. I looked at it and him for a moment, wondering what it would feel like to hold it, to be part of a family. The tears streamed down my face as I carefully placed my hand in his, cautious. I still wasn't sure I could trust him, but I wanted to desperately.

"Maddie's death was not your fault."

"Was it yours? Could you have stopped it?" I looked into his eyes, willing him to tell me the truth.

"No." He said it simply, but it was anything but a simple answer. "I didn't know they were coming until it was done. If we could have done anything to stop them, we would have. I promise."

The resolve in his voice did nothing to quell the anger rising in me. "I don't understand that. You're a mind reader, for God's sake. How could you not know their plan?" I jerked my hand from his.

His frown made the lines in his face deep and harsh. "It is certainly a disturbing turn of events. There is an entire department of the Unseen dedicated to tracking the Potestas. That they didn't see this coming implies the Potestas have developed some new methods. We need time to reveal the true nature of what we're facing."

I sighed, feeling defeated in more ways than one. "Time is all I have left. It's stretching out in front of me like some cruel joke… like it was taken from Maddie and handed to me." Tears threatened, making my voice thick.

"I don't agree. I'm here for you, as are the rest of the Unseen, if you want us for your family."

Silence reigned in the room for a few heartbeats. David, my father, broke the silence first. "What will you do now?"

I looked up at him, thinking of my mother and him, of Maddie and the Potestas. The rage burned new, like nothing I'd ever felt before. But then again, I wasn't who I thought I was. I was a new person now, with a new history, and a new future ahead of me.

Maddie's death was unjust, untimely and unthinkable, but it would be avenged. "I will be one of the Unseen." The anger inside me made my voice low and menacing. "And I will make those responsible for the destruction of my family pay."

Owen was waiting for me outside David's office. He silently took my hand and led me upstairs to the piano. Sitting next to me on the bench, his hand rested warmly on my knee as it bounced on the pedals. I imagined Maddie leaning against the edge of the piano, tapping her foot to the music, humming along. I would always keep her with me. *Gaspard de la Nuit* flowed from my fingers to the keys, to the hammers, to the strings, filling the small room with music, with peace. It was peace I desperately needed at this moment.

I was no longer alone at the piano.

Did you enjoy this book?
Let the author know!
Leave a review!

The following is an excerpt from Stephanie Erickson's dystopian novel, The Cure. Get it online at Amazon, Barnes and Nobel, iTunes, Kobo and Google Play today!

1

"I gladly sacrifice my life for the good of others. One life will make the difference, and that life could be mine. For this reason, I'm devoted to finding the cure." I said the words out loud, but I wasn't thinking about them. A couple of squirrels chasing each other held my attention more securely than the pledge we'd been forced to say since kindergarten. By tenth grade, the thing had lost all meaning.

I sat back down among the rows of desks, still eyeing the squirrels. I folded one of my legs under me and let the other one swing. At five foot three, I wasn't the tallest member of my class, but I wasn't the shortest either. My violet eyes followed the dance of the squirrels while I toyed absently with a lock of my jet-black hair.

My teacher was blabbing about our latest reading assignment, but those dang squirrels were so cute I couldn't focus on her.

"Macey?"

I turned to face her. She was one of the younger members of the faculty, but dressed to try and fit in. Her loose-fitting floral print blouse was tucked into her high-waisted navy skirt. She stared at me over half-glasses perched at the end of her nose. I imagined she referred to them as spectacles and liked to put the end of them into her mouth while pondering literary stuff.

"Hmm?" I asked.

"Care to answer the question?"

I glanced out the window to curse the squirrels, but they were gone. "Could you repeat the question?"

She half-smiled as she leaned against the front of her desk, knowing she'd caught me. "Certainly. Why do you think Billy has a stutter?"

"Oh jeeze, I don't know. I didn't understand a single page of this book, Mrs. Whitehead." A few snickers escaped from some of my classmates. "Hey, guys, don't throw me under the bus here! I couldn't have been the only one who didn't get anything from this!" A few faces turned to Mrs. Whitehead and nodded. "Look, I know this was the shortest thing we've read so far, but it was all moon language to me. Quite frankly, I hated it and think it was a waste of time." I nodded to accentuate my point.

A couple of kids clapped, but soon it died down under Mrs. Whitehead's unceasing gaze. The bitter taste of regret worked its way to the back of my throat. It burned a little like a vurp.

Mrs. Whitehead frowned. "Fair enough. Let's go over it, then, and maybe you'll get more out of it."

Even after talking about it for the next hour, I still didn't get it. I mean, Mrs. Whitehead seemed to find *Billy Budd* very enlightening, and if all that was in there, great. I didn't see it. Sometimes I wondered if people overanalyzed a book. Maybe the writer didn't really mean all that stuff, and you saw something that wasn't meant to be there, ya know? In this case we'd never know. Melville had been dead over two hundred years, so asking him wasn't really an option.

When the bell rang, I gathered my things quickly, hoping to escape the classroom without confrontation. With her gaze burning a hole in the back of my head, I kept my eyes glued to the floor. I was pretty sure her spectacles magnified her stare, the way the sun's heat is more intense through a magnifying glass. I reached up to scratch my scalp, making sure she hadn't given me a bald spot. I rounded the front row of desks and, by some miracle, made it out into the hall where I disappeared among the sea of bodies.

Once I was a safe distance from Mrs. Whitehead's room, I leaned against a row of lockers. *One of these days you should really learn to hold your tongue,* I thought. I took a deep breath, checked the top of my head one more time, and continued on to my next class: History.

Mr. Garvillick was explaining the American Revolution to us. "It was a unique time in history," he said. He tossed his salt-and-pepper hair out of his eyes with a flick of his head. I thought if he kept his comb-over a little shorter it wouldn't be in his eyes in the first place, but then part of his bald head might show.

"The Americans rose up against their perceived oppressors, and..." He searched for the right word. "Well, they won their freedom." Freedom was such an archaic term to me. We still lived in what was known as

America and were told we had our freedoms, but there was so much control, all in the name of the cure. So many had died that no one thought twice when our freedoms were claimed alongside our family members by the disease.

A mousey girl in the front row snapped me back to the discussion. "Mr. Garvillick, what is this picture on the bottom of page 332?"

I flipped ahead to that page to see what she was questioning. There was a rectangle with a dark blue square speckled with white spots in the top left corner, and horizontal red and white stripes were displayed in the bottom left corner of the page. The image was small, a mere column of text in width. Mystified, I stared openly at the picture. I'd never seen anything like it before.

"Oh, that." He cleared his throat. "That's nothing, just their flag. They became unnaturally obsessed with it, and many years later when a more sensible government took over, they removed the symbol in the interest of…well, because it was the right thing to do."

He moved on rather quickly from that topic, not entertaining any more questions about the flag. I didn't hear the rest of the discussion, though. I was captivated by the image. Looking closer at it, I decided the white speckles were stars, arranged in the shape of a circle. And what was a flag?

At lunch, I took out my tablet and punched flag into the search bar.

No results found

It glared defiantly at me. I wondered if the term was so old that it wasn't in the database, or if it was blocked, considered information that was too "charged" for the general population—whatever that meant.

By the end of the day, I was obsessed with the flag. I used my art class as a release. Art was my favorite class. I liked to think of myself as somewhat of an artist, as much as you can in tenth grade. Someday, I wanted to be a professional artist, and have people pay me for my art. Wouldn't that be something? For today, we were doing a still life with watercolors to be graded on technique.

The cream-colored bowl of fruit was placed on a faux oak table in the center of the room. Our tables were arranged around it so we could all have an unobstructed view of the piece. There were about fifteen of us in this class, which wasn't as many as some of my other classes, but Ms. Paige liked to keep her class sizes down to give attention to all her students.

Dutifully, I painted the bowl with its banana, apples, oranges, and a bunch of grapes draped over the side. The table wasn't even draped with an interesting cloth. I sighed. Although my painting looked just like the table in front of me, it was dull. Before I knew it, the flag came flowing from my brush. I watched the background of the painting fill with red, white and blue. Apparently, I'd decided to depict the flag as though it was waving in the breeze, although I had no idea if flags actually did that or what they were used for. It just gave the image some depth.

When I was done, I sat back in my chair, proud of the finished product. The bell rang at least an hour before I finished, but my teacher was used to having me hang behind.

She walked over to see my latest creation. Ms. Paige was what we all called a hippie. She usually had some sort of hemp on her somewhere, whether it was a bracelet or a necklace. I swear one time she came in with a hemp skirt. Her clothes were baggy and generally stained with the remnants of her latest project. For some reason, she liked to wear long beaded necklaces, but they were always dragging in her paints, so the beads didn't all seem to be their original colors anymore. Her brown, frizzy hair was something of a phenomenon. Some of the kids took bets on how long it'd been since she'd washed it. I didn't participate. First of all, there was no way to win. How on earth would they find concrete evidence of that? Second, I liked Ms. Paige. I wasn't interested in berating her. Yeah, she was different, but she's an artist. What did you expect?

"Oh, Macey. I'm sorry, but I can't accept this." She picked up my painting, and I reached out for it instinctively, not sure all the paint was dry.

I took it from her hands, inspecting it for flaws. "What? Why?"

"I just can't. It's too...controversial. You'll have to do it over, or take an F on the project."

I started to protest. "But-"

"I'm sorry Macey. That's my final ruling. Take it or leave it."

She walked back to her office, leaving me, mouth agape, at my station. An F? I'd never gotten an F for anything before, let alone in my favorite class.

I studied the painting closely. The technique wasn't perfect, per se, but it was worth at least a B, and seeing as it was better than all the other kids in the class, it was really worth an A. The project was supposed to be graded on technique.

I blotted the paper with a tissue, making sure it was totally dry, rolled it up, secured it with a piece of twine, grabbed my things, and headed out the door.

This was a first. I never left my art class so bewildered before.

2

I left school totally depressed. Art was subjective. I didn't know anyone who got an F on anything in Art, as long as they put in the effort. That's why it was such a popular class! It was considered an easy A, and here I was, facing an F.

My feet followed their route automatically as I twirled the twine securing my F-worthy painting. Maybe I would ask Alex; he might know what was so bad about it. Alex was two years older than me and studying to be an architect, not an artist, but maybe he knew about these things. But asking him would require telling him what had happened. I wasn't sure I wanted that embarrassment. 'Oh, by the way, your best friend and aspiring artist is looking at taking an F in Art if she doesn't redo her latest project.' I knew he wouldn't laugh at me. Alex never did that. But he might be disappointed—a fate I considered worse than death. I thought about my baby brother, claimed by the disease, and reconsidered. Okay, maybe not *worse* than death, but darn close.

The construction site was only about two miles from school. They were building another housing complex or something. I wasn't really paying close attention when Alex told me. He graduated last year ahead of his class and was working as a contractor to pay for his tuition at the local trade school for architectural design. It was hard labor, but Alex was built for it. Muscular and tan, he never seemed bothered by getting his hands dirty.

We'd been friends since I could remember, long before Joey died, it seemed. He lived up the street from us as a ward of our neighbors. The District paid them to take care of him. He was lucky. They treated him well. Not warmly, but he had everything he needed. He always said he never felt like they were family, not like our family did, but he was grateful to them. Some wards ended up one step above homeless while the families kept all the money the District gave them and spent it on themselves. The disease claimed Alex's family one by one. His dad died from the quest for the cure when Alex was about two, and his mom died from the disease right after he was born. Since then, Alex lived with our neighbors, at least until he started school last fall and got an apartment of his own.

I approached the site and spotted him standing up after setting a couple of two-by-fours on the pile. Outfitted in his normal construction attire, jeans and a white t-shirt, he stretched his back, removed his hard hat, and ran a hand through his blond hair.

I pointed my rolled-up *F* at him. "Ya know, that gold-on-gold look isn't really working out for you. Maybe you should think about dying your hair a different color." I snickered. "Or you could wear makeup to lighten your skin."

"Whatever," he said, and took me in a headlock before releasing me. "What do you want, ya little brat?" He noticed my painting and snatched it from me before I could react.

"I wish you wouldn't."

He started to unfold it. "Why not? You're going to be famous some day, and I'd like to think it will be a portrait of a gold-on-gold Greek God that will make it happen for you." When he saw what it was, his demeanor changed immediately. "Oh. Hey now, Macey. You can't be painting stuff like this." He rolled it up quickly and glanced around, checking for people nearby. Handing it back to me, he asked, "What did your teacher say?"

I shifted my weight and avoided his eyes. "She said if I didn't redo it, I'd get an F on the project." I said it quietly, and some of it was drowned out by the hammering that surrounded us.

"She said what?"

I looked up at him. Although I couldn't see, I just knew his blue eyes were challenging me behind those dark glasses. "She said I'd have to take an F on the project if I didn't redo it."

He tilted his head. "I get the impression you're considering not redoing it."

"Well, look at it!" I offered it back to him, but he didn't take it from me. Instead he glanced back and forth, making sure no one was watching us. I sighed. "Alex, it's good. The project was supposed to be graded on technique. It's not perfect, but I'd be willing to bet it's the best in the class."

Taking a deep breath, he reached for the painting and unrolled it. "It really is quite special, Mace, but you can't turn this in."

"I don't understand why." Tears started welling, and I forced them back. I didn't like to cry, let alone in front of Alex. Crying was for babies and invalids. I was neither of those things. The headache I gained was the reward for my efforts. A battle scar I always wore with pride and without complaint.

"Mace, where did you even see something like that?" He pointed to the flag.

"I saw it in our history book. I don't understand why it's so bad. It was in our book, for heaven's sake."

"What did your history teacher say about it?"

"Just that it was a symbol that people got overly attached to, so the government took it away."

I followed him across the site to the cooler where he grabbed a bottle of water. He sat down and nodded. "Yeah, I guess that's about the gist of it."

"So, if that's all there is to it, why does this deserve an F?"

His blue eyes looked deeply into my own. I hated it when he did that. He knew I was powerless against that stare, only because I could tell he meant business and I didn't want to let him down. "Did you think about what might have caused the government to ban this symbol in the first place? Or even that the symbol is banned? What do you think might happen to you if someone at the Facility got a hold of this?"

I snorted. "Well, I think the people at the Facility are a little busy trying to find that ever-elusive cure to care much about what a tenth-grader paints in Art."

"You're missing the point. Once you turn this stuff in, it stays with you. It doesn't just disappear. It will follow you forever. No one will let you into their school, no one will hire you. You'd be too much of a risk. Too much of a loose cannon."

"Why, though? It's just a painting. And a darn good one at that!" I looked longingly at the painting. Why was it so wrong to be proud of it?

"Hey, Bowman! Break's over! We've got a lot to finish up here!" a man called across the construction yard.

Alex handed the painting back to me. "Yeah! Ok!" he hollered back. "I gotta get back to work. Listen, whatever you decide on this one, please don't paint stuff like this for school again, okay? It's just not...constructive."

"Yeah, I guess." I wasn't sure I agreed with him. How could it not be constructive to express myself? Although, when I really thought about it, I didn't know what exactly I was expressing with the painting. Why did it have to have such a controversial meaning behind it? Why couldn't it just be a beautiful painting? That was all I meant it as. Maybe if I explained that to the teacher she'd accept it. I frowned, doubting my conclusion.

On my walk home, I looked at my neighborhood with new eyes. What about that stupid flag had made it the way it was? On the surface, everything seemed fine, which was by design. The streets were well-manicured, although not fancy. Trees were evenly spaced and all the same height, homes were equal distances apart and all the same. Everything, down to the frequency of grass cutting was tightly controlled to maintain a uniform and "clean" appearance. The government said it provided fewer distractions, and thus would help lead them to a cure faster. My mom commented once before Joey died that it had turned into a "Stepford community" overnight, but

Dad shushed her before I could ask what that meant.

What did it look like when the flag and the freedom it represented existed? Were the homes different colors? Different shapes? Different sizes? Did everyone choose what their lawns looked like? Was the image really that distracting? Growing up with such uniformity, the image was difficult to picture, but I couldn't imagine something so minute was all that damaging.

As I turned the corner and walked down yet another identical street, I thought about just redoing the project. I mean, I had the likeness of the fruit in my original painting. It wouldn't take me very long to do it. It was just the principle of the thing. Why should I redo something that met the requirements of the project? I shouldn't. It was as simple as that.

Resolved, I walked up the driveway to our home. It looked exactly like all the other homes in this neighborhood, right down to the two sycamore trees in the front yard. We weren't the first family to live in it and probably wouldn't be the last, but for now, it was ours. That made it perfect to me.

The pale yellow siding always greeted me with a smile. Rosie unlocked the front door when I approached.

I stood in the doorway as she sanitized me, making sure the disease didn't come inside. "Welcome home, Macey." She said in her soothing but still robotic voice as the beam covered me in a green glow. It wasn't as sophisticated or intense as the one we had at school, but I guessed it didn't need to be. That one was super high-powered and worked much faster. It was meant for higher volume. Here at home, Rosie only had the three of us to keep healthy.

"Hey, Rosie. What's new?"

"Your arrival at home." She always answered the same way, but I still asked because some part of me found it funny.

Rosie was what we named our home. Mom said it was a reference to some cartoon from the twentieth century, but I never figured out which one. Rosie was an automated system, the latest technology when the house was built, but now pretty outdated. She suited our needs, though.

I tossed my backpack on the stairs and parked myself on the couch. "Rosie, are Mom and Dad on their way home yet?"

"Your mother is seven minutes and forty-two seconds away from home. Your father is still at work."

Satisfied, I unrolled the painting and rested it against the red glass vase that lived in the middle of the coffee table. Leaning back on the couch, I studied my work.

The colors were perfect. Lines, a little shaky, but getting better. Proportions, right on the money. These were the things I was told we'd be graded on. The more I thought about it, the more I felt this was the piece I would turn in. Convinced my teacher would change her mind once she'd had time to think about it logically, I folded my arms over my chest, pleased with my accomplishment.

My resolve wavered, though, when I heard the garage door, signaling the arrival of my mom.

BIBLIOGRAPHY

Home Page. *spdfoundation.net*. 2014. The Sensory Processing
Disorder Foundation. 12 September 2014.
<http://spdfoundation.net/about-sensory-processing-disorder.html>

"How Music Helps to Heal the Injured Brain."
www.brainline.org. 2010. The Dana Foundation. 12
September 2014.
<http://www.brainline.org/content/2011/03/
how-music-helps-to-heal-the-injured-brain.html>

"Music Therapy: The Healing Power of Music."
Musictherapyintheus.wordpress.com. 12 September 2014.
<http://musictherapyintheus.wordpress.com/success-stories/>

"What is ILS?" *www.integratedlistening.com*. 2014. 12
September 2014.
<http://www.integratedlistening.com/parents/what-is-ils/>.

ACKNOWLEDGMENTS

First and foremost, I thank God for everything. For giving me the words, time, and drive to complete this project. I am in constant awe of the blessings I've received recently, and my gratitude in increasingly inadequate.

Although *Unseen* is my third published book, for me, it's a first of sorts. It's the first book I'm publishing as a full-time author. It's scary, exciting, and uncomfortably real. Through the rollercoaster, my husband has been such an amazing supporter, cheerleader, business partner, best friend, and general cohort. It's because of him that this book even came to be. Honey, your support with this endeavor is so appreciated! I'm so excited to see how far we can take it!

Of course, no project can come together without the unrelenting support of your team. So, I'd like to first thank my amazing editors Angela and Cynthia. Angela, you really got out your turd polish on this one and helped me take Unseen from an okay story to something I am so freaking excited about! Cynthia, I thank you for removing every misplaced comma, every extra space, every wrongly used word, and other sinful grammatical errors. And who can forget the beta readers? My favorite beta, Jamie, is an amazingly patient person who can read a barely passable draft and point out glaring errors while still making you feel like it's amazing enough to keep going. What would I do without you?

No book is completed without friends and family. Sometimes they end up as characters in the book, sometimes they sit on the sidelines, quietly supportive while you write just one more chapter, but they're always there, always interested and always excited. Dannie and Mary, you guys are amazing. I love you both so much and hope I can be as good to you as you are to me.

My parents are a force to be reckoned with. Their support for whatever I do is ceaseless, loud, and joyful. I know I'm lucky to have such selfless people for my parents, and hope that if you don't, dear reader, you have at least one person in your life who can show you what unconditional love looks like.

Lastly, of course, a book is nothing but a paperweight without a reader. So, I thank *you*. You've taken hours from your busy schedule to spend time with my characters, and me. I know what a sacrifice that is, believe me, and I am so grateful. I certainly enjoyed it, and I hope you did too! Until next time!

–S

ABOUT THE AUTHOR

Stephanie Erickson is an English Literature graduate from Flagler College. She lives in Florida with her family. Unseen is her third novel.

Stephanie loves to connect with readers! Follow her on Facebook at http://www.facebook.com/stephmerickson, Twitter @sm_erickson.

Check out her Web site at www.stephanieericksonbooks.com where you can catch up on the latest news and coming events. Be sure to sign up for the newsletter while you're there, and you'll be the first to hear about new releases, upcoming promotions and more!